KB085301

당신에 대해서

도서출판 아시아에서는 《바이링궐 에디션 한국 대표 소설》을 기획하여 한국의 우수한 문학을 주제별로 엄선해 국내외 독자들에게 소개합니다. 이 기획은 국내외 우수한 번역가들이 참여하여 원작의 품격을 최대한 살렸습니다. 문학을 통해 아시아의 정체성과 가치를 살피는 데 주력해 온 도서출판 아시아는 한국인의 삶을 넓고 깊게 이해하는 데 이 기획이 기여하기를 기대합니다.

Asia Publishers presents some of the very best modern Korean literature to readers worldwide through its new Korean literature series 〈Bilingual Edition Modern Korean Literature〉. We are proud and happy to offer it in the most authoritative translation by renowned translators of Korean literature. We hope that this series helps to build solid bridges between citizens of the world and Koreans through a rich in-depth understanding of Korea.

바이링궐 에디션 한국 대표 소설 043

Bi-lingual Edition Modern Korean Literature 043

On You

이인성
당신에 대해서

Yi In-seong

ASIA
PUBLISHERS

Contents

당신에 대해서

On You

우선, 이 소설을 읽으려는 당신에게, 잠깐 동안 눈을 감도록 권하겠다.

  눈을 감지 않고 위의 비어 있는 한 줄을 뛰어넘었다면, 제발, 아래의 비어 있는 한 줄을 건너기 전에, 꼭, 눈을 감아보기 바란다. 이때 눈을 감고 무엇을 어떻게 할지는, 전적으로, 또한 기필코, 당신 자신이 깨달아내야 할 일이다. 그러니 앞에서 눈을 감았었더라도 그저 눈꺼풀을 덮어본 놀음에 불과했다면, 이 경우 역시, 다시 한 번 당신 눈 속의 그 어둠과 마주하는 게 스스로 뜻깊겠다. 이번엔 가능한 한 오랫동안, 눈꺼풀 안으로 쫓아

First, before you set out to read this story, I sug-
gest you close your eyes for a moment.

If it so happened that you skipped the blank line
above without closing your eyes, then please, before you reach the empty space below, try to just
close your eyes for a moment. What, exactly, you
do with your eyes closed in this moment, and how
you do it, is a question that you must—overall, and
necessarily—answer yourself. So even if you did
close your eyes before, if it was nothing more than
playing at covering a ball with lid, then now, too, a
second encounter with the darkness behind those
same eyes may prove meaningful for you. This

들어온 현란한 빛 무늬가 완전히 암흑의 뒤편으로 스러지도록. 그래서 원컨대, 그 짙은 어둠의 응시가 이 소설 읽기를 지탱하도록.

분명, 당신은 눈을 감지 않았거나 너무 일찍 눈을 떴다. 그렇다면, 그러므로, 이제 이 순간, 돌연히, "오, 빌어먹을! 늘 똥 마려운 듯한 그대, 성급한 독자여! 속물이여! 개새끼여!"라는 격한 욕설—써놓고 나니 지나치게 시적이다—을 당신에게 퍼부어버려도 상관은 없으리라. 용기 있게 그랬던 그 누군가들처럼. 그러나, 그렇게 강풍처럼 당신을 몰아치는 것이 결코 무턱댄 짓은 아니더라도, 그러나, 현재의 나—나? 나, 누구?—로서는 그러고 싶은 생각이 전혀 없다. 다름 아닌 당신에 대해 당신에게 이야기하기 위해서는, 지금 여기서, 끝끝내 당신을 끌어안아야만 하겠기 때문에. 아니, 아무래도 '전혀'라는 말은 좀 거짓이다. 죄송하다. 게다가 글이란 대개 순서적으로 읽히는 것이니까, 앞서의 문장들에서 당신은, '그러나'의 반전이 일어나기 전까지 잠깐 동안, 이미 약간의 불쾌한 충격을 느꼈음직하다. 솔직히 이야기해, 이런 시대—어떤 시대?—를 함께 살면서, 그 미풍

time, keep your eyes shut for as long as possible, until the last fantastic patterns of light that have slipped inside your eyelids fade completely to black. The hope, here, is that comtemplating this deep darkness might sustain your reading of this story.

To be sure, you either didn't close your eyes at all or opened them too soon. Because that was the case, therefore, right now, in this instant, I trust it wouldn't matter now were I to suddenly shower you with curses: "Oh, damnation! Oh, hasty reader, always rushing ahead like you're holding your bowels! You philistine! You son of a dog!" (Downright poetic these words are, now that I've written them.) Just like those whoevers, who so bravely hurled curses at their readers. But then again, even if coming at you like some gale force wind wouldn't, in fact, be a misstep, the thing is, the I—me? me, who?—of this moment has no desire at all to do any such thing. In order to speak to you—and not just anyone—on the subject of you, what I must do here and now is draw you into my arms and hold you to the bitter end. Although, actually, saying "no desire *at all*" is a bit of a lie. I'm sorry. And since

같은 충격조차 빼버리고 싶지는 않았다고나 할까. 이 마음이 당신에게 이해되기를. 지금 당장은 아니더라도 그 언젠가는.

　그렇다, 그 '그 언젠가'를 향해 막막히 이 소설은 시작되고 있다. 아마도 멀고먼 그 언젠가, 당신을 다르게 참답게 만나겠다는 마음을 꾸면서. 하지만 그 언젠가가 아닌 지금의 당신은, 오히려 이런 내 태도에 대해 반발하고 싶은 것이 아닐까? 어쩌면 이런 식으로 나를 비웃고 싶을는지도 모른다. "미풍 같은 불쾌감은커녕 입김 같은 느낌도 없는걸." 뭐, 더 심하게, "좆같은 새끼, 지랄하고 자빠졌네. 지가 뭔데 남을 갖고 놀라구 그래?" 하는 소리―써놓고 나니 이건 상당히 사실적인 욕이다―가 들려올 듯도 하다. 그건 필경, 뭣도 못 되는 내가 건네주는 시늉만 했던 쬐끄만 욕사발을 당신이 지레짐작, 미리 낚아채 얻어 마신 덕분에 토해내는 욕지기일 터이다(그래도 이렇게나마 반발감을 느낀다면, 역설적이지만 한 줄기 희망이 있다?―애매한 질문이 불쑥 괄호 안에 묶여 튀어나온다). 여기서(거기서), 추상적으로 역할 그 욕지기의 냄새를 추상적으로나마 직접 맡고 확인할 수 없다고 해서 (왜 그런지 언뜻 대답을 구할 수 없는 의문 자체로밖에 구체화될

words are usually read in the order they appear, it seems possible that you may have already experienced a bit of an unpleasant shock before coming upon the twist presented in the "but" in the few sentences previous. Were I to be perfectly honest, however, I might say that living as we are in this day and age—which day and age?—I was reluctant to forfeit completely, to let go of that gentle breeze of a tiny shock. I can only hope that you understand this stance. If not right now, then, at least, someday.

Yes, it is towards this same 'someday' that this story begins, blindly striding forth. Nurturing the idea that on this far, far away someday, you and I will meet again differently, and in truth. But then is it also possible that, not yet being the you of this someday, the you of now might actually wish to resist this attitude of mine? Perhaps you simply feel the urge to mock me, as such: "A 'gentle breeze of a tiny shock'? Please. Doesn't even have the impact of a breath." Or, who knows, maybe go a bit stronger: "What an absolute dick, what a load of bullshit. Who does he think he is, trying to play with people?" It's like I can almost hear you saying the words. (Words which, now that I've written them, seem

수 없다고 해서), 나는(당신은), 얼마든지 그럴 수도 있으리라는 투로 한 발자국 물러서는 일종의 자기 속임수를 쓰지는 않겠다(마찬가지로, 생각해보니 그런대로 재미있을 것도 같은 소설인데—하고 슬쩍 얼버무리고픈 함정에서 벗어나야 된다). 차라리 적극적으로(그러면 당연히), 나는(당신은), 그것을 일단 긍정적인 사건으로 받아들이려 하는데(이 태도의 또 다른 위험성에 대해서도 새로운 의혹을 뒤잇게 될 텐데), 왜냐하면 이제 그 비어버린 허구의 욕사발을 물끄러미 응시하는 당신을 상상하면서(왜냐하면 그렇게 당신을 상상하는 나를 상상하면서), 그 모습이, 그 비어 있음을 통해 바로 당신 자신을 보고 있다고 판단하기 때문이다(정말 그러한지, 모든 물음들을 당신 자신에게 되돌리는 의식의 시련 속에 빠져들 수밖에 없겠기 때문이다). 내 상상 속에서, 당신은, 당신 자신을 바라보는 그런 자세로, 이 소설에 대한 순종을 거부하고 있는 것이다(당신은, 얼마나 오랫동안, 당신을 거꾸로 덮치는 말사발 속에, 환한 듯 캄캄하게 갇혀들곤 했던가). 어쩌다 입장은 대립되었었지만, 어쨌든 당신도 당신 나름의 길을 따라 '그 언젠가'에 이르고 싶다는 듯이(부디 그러기를!).

앞뒤가 그리 짜여질 수 있다면, 이제, 그 반발의 방식

quite appropriate, as insults go.)

After all, what's happening here is that I, yes, little old me, am pretending to dish out a handful of insults that you, in anticipation, have already snatched up and swallowed whole, allowing this current regurgitation. (And if, at least, this sense of rebellion persists, perhaps there is still the possibility—though somewhat paradoxical—of hope? An ambiguous question making an abrupt appearance anchored by parantheses.) Here (there), just because the offensive stink of these insults cannot be directly—albeit, abstractly—smelled and confirmed (or because the reason why can only be rendered specific in the quandary of its very unanswerability), I (you) will not take refuge in the stance that this reaction is certainly understandable and will not step back in what would essentially be an act of self-deception. (In the same vein, it is vital to avoid the trap of simply equivocating, of surrendering to the notion that, come to think of it, this might itself make for an interesting story). Indeed, it would be preferable for me (you) to try and enthusiastically (and so naturally) accept this whole incident as a positive one (acknowledging the inevitability of doubts regarding the possible new dangers of this stance in its turn), because when I now imagine you gazing blankly upon that empty,

으로 당신에 대한 당신 자신을 더 깊이—아니, 그런즉, 더 표면적으로—바라보는 것에는, 당신도 동의해줄 수 있지 않을까? 욕지기를 뱃속까지 뒤집어 훑어내고 나서 제 몸을 납작하게 뻗쳐 눕힌 마음으로, 최초의 당신이 보일 때까지. 처음의 제안과는 정반대로, 두 눈을 부릅뜨고. 자, 그렇다면……, 그렇듯 두 눈에 온 힘을 모으고, 그리고 다음 한 줄의 빈 공간 앞에서 읽기를 멈추고, 수시로 잊어버릴 테지만 끊임없이 되돌아와야 할 자리인 지금 그 상태의 당신을, 살살이, 둘러보라.

보았는가, 바로 지금 거기서 이 소설을 앞에 둔 당신 자신을? 그래서 솟구쳐 알겠는가, 이제는 나에 대한 맹목적인 부정도 거두어야 한다는 것을? 가령 앞 문단의 첫머리에서 "나는 오랫동안 눈을 감고 있었거니와 스스로 모든 것을 알고 넘어섰는데 웬 시비냐?"라고 당신이 항의한들, 이 소설을 계속 읽어나가는 데는 헛물켜는 짓이나 다름없음을. 그리고 알겠는가, 그렇다고 나에 대한 맹목적의 긍정으로 단순히 돌아와서도 안 된다는 것을? 가령 내가 뒤이어 당신의 반응을 적절히 지적해 냈다고 해서 새삼 "그렇지, 그래." 하고 고개를 끄덕인

16

meaningless bundle of insults (because I am imagining myself imagining you), this sight of you, I judge that through that very emptiness you are, in fact, looking upon yourself (because the question of whether this is, in fact, true, and all such related questions, when turned back upon you, would inevitably lead you to an inescapable trial of consciousness). In the realm of my imagination, you, assuming a posture of self-reflection, are refusing to acquiesce to this unfolding story (and as for you, what long stretches of time you have found yourself shut up in the darkness, by turns almost illuminating, of these torrential, swooping words, that have been knocking you off your feet). As if to say, true, somewhere along the line we have been pitted against one another, but you, too, still hope to follow your own path to reach that same *someday* (I hope you do!).

If both sides, then, can be put together in such a way, this mode of resistance might become a means of examining you on the subject of you more deeply—or, in other words, more superficially—can we perhaps agree, at least, on this? Flip your stomach inside out and scrape up and expel all the nausea within, stretch your body out and lay down flat, embrace this mindset until you can see the very first you. And now, the opposite of that

들, 이번엔 뜨물 먹고 주정하는 짓이 된다는 것을. 그래서 또 한 번 솟구쳐 알겠는가, 색깔 다른 두 마리 뱀—살갗에 비늘이 돋혀오는 징그러움의 홀연한 아름다움, 그 상투적 느낌과 껴안는 새로움!—이 서로서로 꼬리를 물고 돌게 하며 그 가운데의 낯선 공간을 우리의 그 '무엇'으로 빚어내야 하는 알 마음의 노동을?…… 그래도 아직 모르겠는가, 이 비약 아닌 비약들을?……

 이런, 이런 세상에……. 느닷없는 충동에 겨워 단박 끝장이라도 볼 듯한 질문들을 쏟아놓고 나니, 시작의 한 고비로는 너무 숨가쁘다. 그것도 암담하기 그지없는 숨가쁨. 특히 마지막 질문이 덧붙여진 순간은, 갑자기 내가 나에게 당한 듯이 허망하게 무너지는 기분이었다. 당신의 대답이 전혀 들리지 않았으니까……. 뭐? 당신의 대답이 들리지 않았다고? 그럼, 방금 내가 당신의 대답을 즉각적으로 듣고야 말겠다는 심산으로 그 질문들을 퍼부었단 말인가? 두말할 나위 없이 당연한 결과가 초래되리라는 것도 잊고?…… 바보 같으니! 지금 여기서 당신의 대답을 판별해낼 수 없음은, 뭐랄까, 애당초 절대적인, 그리고 끝끝내 돌이킬 수 없는, 그래서 죽음처럼 숙명적인 현실이요 조건이 아닌가. 마치 지금 거

first request: open both your eyes wide, as if to say, Okay, here we go. Gather all the pressure into your two eyes, stop reading, focus on the space in the empty line below, and then, gently, look around at the you in this very moment, in this state, this state that will be forgotten again and again without end, but a state that you must also return to innumerable times.

Did you see, just there, just now, the you waiting for this story to begin? And are you overcome with the understanding that now you must put aside this blind negativity towards me? Even supposing that at the start of this paragraph you protested, saying "Not only did I keep my eyes closed, I also came to understand and overcome everything, so what is all this?" These protests are as effective as bailing water out with a sieve in terms of moving this story forward.

And do you see, too, that simply turning the other way to embrace a blind positivity towards me would be just as unacceptable? Even supposing that you have been nodding along all this time, murmuring "Yes, yes, that's it exactly," to every reaction of yours I've pointed out so far—this attitude

기 있는 당신이, 지금 여기 있는 내 육체의 호흡이 갑자기 거칠어져 있는 사실을 감지할 수는 없듯이. 이것은 다름 아닌 소설이므로. 지금, 나는 소설을 쓰고 있는 것이다. 지금, 나는 당신과 만나 목소리를 나누고 있지 않은 것이다. 그런데 그 모든 것을 알고 있었으면서도, 불현듯 솟구치고 싶은 욕망 때문에—그 욕망 자체야 하등 탓할 바가 있으랴만—마음결만 소용돌이에 휘말린 셈이다. 더구나 이 어쩔 수 없음이야말로 실제로는 그 고동치던 질문들의 근거이기조차한데, 이렇게 글의 머리와 꼬리를 뒤바꿔버린 꼴 하며…… 그래, 여기선 불가능한 당신의 확정적인 대답을 구하지 않는 글길을 따라갔어야 했다. 더 앞에서는 이미 그럴 듯하게 해냈던 것처럼. 그리고 이 지점에서 '왠지 알겠는가? 바로 이게 소설이기 때문이 아니겠는가?'라는 식의 글 형식을 취할 수 있듯이. 하기야 소설이라고 꼭 대놓은 질문을 하지 말란 법은 없겠다. 하지만 그것이 하나의 열린 마무리가 아닐 때, 거기에 다음 순간의 내 독단이나 단호함 혹은 급박한 방향 전환이 요구되는 것은 필연이다. 요컨대 위 질문들을 그대로 뒤이으려면, 나는 당신을 알아들었거나 못 알아들은 어느 한편으로 일방적으로 간주

would still be no different than acting drunk after drinking water instead of wine. So, are you now overcome once more with the understanding of the cost, of the sheer labor of the heart involved in having two different colored snakes—the revulsion of scales sprouting from skin, that unexpected loveliness! the sensation of those tired conventions, the embrace of that newness!—bite one another's tails and spinning and turning this strange space into this very *something* of ours? Do you still not see, these leaps that are anything but leaps?

Oh, oh goodness... Now that I've let loose this barrage of questions, as if I needed answers right away (the result of having succumbed to an abrupt impulse, no more), what should have been just the crux of a long beginning has left me breathless. And the darkest kind of breathless, too. And asking that final question in particular, it felt as though I had been brought down by my own hand, that all had been in vain. Because, you see, I couldn't hear your answer at all... What's that? Couldn't hear your answer at all, is that right? Is the suggestion, then, that these questions just now were all leveled at you with the secret desire of receiving a certain, and immediate response? That I've conveniently

21

하거나, 이야기의 다른 매듭으로 건너뛰어야만 한다. 그러나 그렇게 가파라지기에는 아직 자리가 마땅치 않다. 그러니 어리석은 나여, 아무래도 여기선 내 가쁜 숨이나 얼른 가다듬는 게 낫겠다.

그 사이, 엉겁결에 허둥지둥 내 글의 숨결을 뒤쫓아왔을 당신도, 멈춰서서 내 횡설수설의 타당성을 한번 따져볼 일이다.

이유 없이 하나의 영상이 떠오른다. 어떤 짙은 어둠의 집 밖으로 막 나서서 눈부심에 눈물겨운 눈을 찡그리며 주춤거리는, 그러나 빛 속을 건너보기 위해 고통스럽게 초점을 찾는 나어린 누군가의 모습이. 언제 어디선가 본 것만 같은데, 누구일까?

이 영상의 심연으로부터도, 지금은 어서 빠져나가야 한다.

천천히, 다시 시작하자. 문제의 첫 질문으로 돌아가서 : 보았는가, 바로 지금 거기서 이 소설을 앞에 둔 당신 자신을? 그러면 무엇을 보았는가, 당신 자신으로부터? 당신의 옷차림을, 당신의 자세를, 당신의 몸 생김새를, 이 책을 붙들고 있는 손 모습을? 또?…… 그리고 그 보

forgotten the fact that any such line of questioning would, of course, lead to eminently knowable results? What an idiot I am! After all, isn't the very inability here to discern your answers an—how shall we put it—an absolute reality, from the first, and ultimately irreversible reality, and therefore a set of conditions as predestined as death itself? Just as you, where you are now, can have no way of knowing the fact that here, where I now am, my breathing has suddenly grown rough, uneven. Because this is a story, no more, no less. Right now, I am writing a story. Right now, I am not sitting with you, we are not sharing voices. And yet, even though I know all of these things, it is as if a sudden surge of desire—a desire that certainly could not be blamed!—has simply swept up my thoughts in a kind of whirlpool. Indeed, the very unavoidability of these answers has, in fact, been the basis of these throbbing questions themselves, bringing me to this reversal of heads and tails when it comes to all these words... It's true, what I should have done was follow a path that did not seek that most impossible thing: your definitive answer. Just as I had managed to more or less accomplish, further back towards the beginning. Just as, now, I am

이는 것 너머로는 무엇을?……

　당연히, 이번엔 당신의 직접적인 대답이 목적은 아니다. 나는 다만, 조금 전 내가 나에게 되풀이 확정되었듯, 무엇보다도 당신이 당신에게 확인되기를 원한다. 이 순간 최소한 확실한 행위의 주체자인 당신으로서, 즉 딴살을 뺀 이 소설의 독자로서. 지금, 당신은 아무튼 읽고 있는 것이다. 지금, 당신은 나와 만나 목소리를 나누고 있지 않은 것이다. 그러나, 그럼에도 불구하고, 여기에 이르기 전까지는, 또 이 이후에도, 때 없이, 당신은 무심코 나와 대화를 주고받는 듯한 착각에 빠져들었거나 빠져들기 쉽다. 여기서도 막바지로, "아, 그럴지도 모르겠다."라는 서술형 대화체로 글 쓰듯 혼자 대꾸하며, 어쩌면 그 역시 이게 소설이기 때문에 오랜 습관을 떨치지 못하고 어쩔 수 없이.

　맹세코, 이건 당신을 비난하려는 태세가 아니다. 나는 오히려 이 착각의 자연스러움을 한편으로 자연스럽게 깨우칠 때, 그러면서 다시 그 자연스러움에 기꺼이 몸담을 때, 그리고도 수시로 거기서 자유롭게 빠져나올 수 있을 때, 그렇게 넘나들 수 있을 때(때, 때, 때, 때, 슬며시 말에 가락이 붙어), 더 드넓은 말밭이 펼쳐지리라는 것

able to adopt the following mode of questioning: "Can you see now? Can you see that it's because what we have here is a story?" Granted, there's no law forbidding the use of direct questions in the course of a story. But then again, when such questions are not open ended, they must necessarily be followed, in the very next instant, by a decision from me, or a resolution, or an urgent change in the narrative direction. In short, if we were to simply keep on with the above line of questioning, I would simply have to consider that you have, or have not understood, one or the other, or else just skipped ahead to a different knot in this story. But the space is not yet right for such a move. And so it would seem, for foolish me, that the best thing to do here is to just take a moment to try and slow my quickened breathing.

Meanwhile, having scrambled along this far with the breath of this prose, it would behoove you, too, to stop here a moment, and reflect on the validity of my ramblings.

An image appears before me for no particular reason. A figure, someone young, emerging from a house submerged in darkness, halting, squinting

을 드러내고 싶을 뿐이다(밭을 가세~ 밭을 가세~). 그 착
각의 소지가, 독자인 당신이 읽는 당신이 내가 그려내
는 바의 당신이라는 사실에 있는 까닭이다(씨 뿌리세~
씨 뿌리세~). 되돌아보라(노래를 끊자, 냉정히). 한 예로, 나
는 당신에 대해서, '분명, 당신은 눈을 감지 않았거나 너
무 일찍 눈을 떴다'고 썼었다. 그리고 그것을 전제로 그
다음 줄거리를 이었다. 하다못해 당신이 어떠어떠하게
반발하리라는 것까지도 임의로 적었다. 하지만 그때그
때, 그 도처에서, 실제의 당신은 그 진술 내용을 벗어나
있었기 십상이다(그동안 당신과 당신에 대한 내 묘사가 완벽
하게 일치해왔다고 행복해하는 사람은 수상하기 짝이 없으니 가
슴에 손을 얹을 것). 그런데 또 한 번 뒤집자면, 다시 그럼
에도 불구하고, 당신이 거기서 여기까지 계속 읽었다는
명백함이 놀라운 것이다. 술집이나 다방의 한구석에 처
음으로 얼굴을 맞대고 앉아 내가 "눈 감어!" "눈 부릅떠!"
를 외치며 다른 사람도 아닌 당신에 대해 일방적 판단
을 늘어놓는 광경 속에서라면, 보나마나 당신은 내 뺨
을 후려쳤거나 미친 놈 피하듯 자리를 떴을 것이다. 헌
데 그와 맞먹는 상황의 문자 재현인 이 소설을 당신은
내팽개치지 않았다(이미 내팽개친 사람은 스스로 나의 '당신'

their watering eyes in the light outside, trying, painfully, to focus their gaze through the brightness. I've seen this somewhere before; who can it be?

We must move fast, we must escape the abyss of this image, for now.

Slowly, let us begin again. Let's return to that first question: Did you see, just now, just here, the you who has this story ahead of you? And what is it you saw, about this particular you? Did you see your clothes, your posture, the look and shape of your body, the sight of you holding this book? Again? ...And maybe something more, something just beyond these visible things?

Naturally, the goal this time is not your direct answer. All I want is for you to confirm yourself in your own eyes, just as I myself have repeatedly confirmed myself in mine. Confirmed, in this moment, being, at the very least, the principle agent involved in a definitive action: if nothing else, you are the reader of this story. Whatever else, right now, you are reading. Right now, you and I are not sharing voices. And yet, despite this, up until this moment, and also after this moment has passed, at any time, it has been, and will be easy to absently

이기를 거절하고 이 글의 세계 밖으로 나갔으니, 지금껏 나의 '당신'인 당신과는 전혀 다른 차원에 존재한다). 왤까? 그것은 당신이 이 소설 앞에 최초로 다가왔던 이전의 당신—이 당신은 어떻게 이루어졌는가—과는 다른 이후의 당신—이 당신은 어떻게 이룩될 것인가—이 되고자 하는 또 하나의 당신과 포개져 있었기 때문이 아닐까? 여섯 살 윤곽이 환갑 얼굴에 어리는 변함없음만큼이나, 여섯 살 수줍쟁이를 환갑 불호랑이로 바꿔놓는 동력이 존재하듯?

이 소설 읽기의 동력인, 또 하나의 당신? 몸이 마주치는 자리에서는 자신의 실증적 표상인 얼굴 때문에 섣불리 나타나지 않는, 이렇게 이런 소설의 '당신'을 용납함으로써나 슬며시 스며나오는, 그러면서도 여전히 어디에 어떻게 포개져 있는지 불확실한, 당신이면서 당신이 아닌, 또 하나의 당신—우선은 그렇게 일컬어두자. 그러면 희미하게나마 의식하겠는가, 당신이 나를 헛보며 소리 없이 말을 되받아 건넨 상대가 실상은 그 또 하나의 당신이었음을. 그리하여 당신의 당신 자신과 나의 '당신'인 당신을 끊임없이 오가는 넓이 속에 부득이 펼쳐진 당신! 여기서 당신은 그중의 한쪽으로 고정될 수

fall into the illusion that you and I are having a conversation. Here, too, a last-ditch response, "Ah, that might indeed be possible," a conversational declarative response, mumbled alone. This is, perhaps, unavoidable; an old habit dying hard: this is, after all, a story.

Truly, my plan of attack here is not to criticize you. Rather, I merely hope to show that when you come to a natural understanding, on the one hand, of the inevitable nature of this illusion, and when this leads to your willing embrace of this inevitable nature, and when, whenever you please, you are able to freely engage and disengage from this embrace (when, when, when, when, the words start to take on a kind of melody), an ever-broader field of words will open up before you (the field we plow~ the field we plow~). The root of this illusion, after all, lies in the overlap between the you that you are reading, as reader, and the you that I am describing (the seeds we sow~ the seeds we sow~). Look back (let us stop singing this song, now; let's be cold). For example, I wrote the following about you: "Guaranteed, you either didn't close your eyes at all or opened them too soon." Then, I went on to use this as the basis for what followed. I even went so far as to arbi-

없다. 그 두 당신을 하나의 당신으로 부르는 나에 의해.

그러므로 만약 이 새로운 어쩔 수 없음이 글읽기의 눈짓 속에 깊이 배어들기를 희망한다면, 당신은, 차후, 적어도 행간을 띄우는 자리에서만은, 의식적으로라도 눈길을 멈추어야만 하리라.

그러고 보니, 나는 벌써부터 당신에 대한—더불어, 불가피하게 당신과의 관계 속에 곁세워진 나에 대한—이야기를 꽤나 진행해 온 셈이다. 당신이 이『한없이 낮은 숨결』이란 소설집을 처음 집어 들었을 때, 목차에 나타난 이 소설의 제목이 터놓고 암시해주었던 대로. 그런데 막상 인사가 너무 늦어진 듯싶다. 무례에 대해 용서를 빌면서, 늦게나마 인사를 드려야겠다.

—독자여, 안녕하셨는가? 나는 이 소설의 작가 이인성이다. 다름 아닌 당신에 대한 소설을 쓰며, 나는 지금…….

인사를 적다가 문득, 나는 지금, 당신이 이 인사법에 주목해주었으면 좋겠다는 생각에 쏠린다. 나는 물론 이 소설의 이야기꾼이지만, 이 소설에선 이야기꾼으로서의 다른 이름을 가지고 있지 않다. 나는 본문 안에서도

trarily note this or that possible protest you might have had. But now and then, at various points, the sentiments of the real you may well have been some distance apart from what I wrote (any person perfectly content with how precisely my descriptions of you have fit you up to this point is an object of utmost suspicion, and ought now to place their hand over their heart). Or, to flip things once more, the fact that you have clearly continued reading to this point in spite of this mismatch between us is downright astonishing. If we had met for the first time in the corner of some bar or café, and I had commenced to sit across from you shouting "Close your eyes!" and "Open them wide!" and then gone on to lay out a panoply of unilateral judgments on, not just any subject, but on you yourself, there is no question that you would have slapped me in the face, or left the bar, avoiding me the way you would any apparent nutcase. And yet, despite the fact that this is the literary reenactment of just such a situation, you have yet to cast this story aside (anyone who has already cast this aside has voluntarily rejected the categorization of the *you* of my address and removed themselves from the world of this story, and therefore exists on a plane completely separate from the *you* of my address that you are on,

여전히 이 책 표지에 인쇄되어 있는 이름의 존재와 동일한 이인성이고자 하는 것이다. 이상하게 들릴지 모르겠는데, 이 점은 퍽 중요하다. 지금, 나는, 그동안 줄곧 그래왔고 앞으로도 대개는 그럴 것이듯이, 내 소설 속에 나오는 다른 이야기꾼이 되기를 애써 피한다.

이 말을, 당신에 대한 또 하나의 당신의 관계와 혼돈해서는 안 된다. 물론, 당신에 대해 그렇게 규정하고 난후, 나에게도 또 하나의 내가 있음이 느껴지기는 느껴진다. 무엇보다도 만년필을 쥔 내 손놀림을 통해. 하지만, 나와 또 하나의 나 사이에서 쓰이는 소설 속, 다른이야기꾼들에 대한 고려는 차원이 바뀐 문제로 보인다. 작가와는 다른 이름으로 무수히 가능한 다른 이야기꾼들이란, 새로운 두께로 겹쳐져, 나로 하여금 바로 나와또 하나의 나 사이를 오가게 하는, 그 사이 속에 개입해들어오는 타인의 얼굴로 다가오는 것이다. 그래서 소설쓰기는 언제나 결단을 부른다. 그 낯익으면서도 낯선무형의 얼굴을 위해 어떤 이름을 붙여줄 것인가? 이름과 함께, 그는 나를 벗어나 독자적인 주체이자 대상이될 테지. 나로부터의 분열이든 확산이든, 그때 하나의실체인 그는 이미 그인 것이다. 그렇지만 오늘, 나는 그

and have been so far). Why? Is it perhaps because there is a you who seeks to become a you of the after—how, I wonder, will you achieved this you—separate from the you who first approached this story—what, I wonder, did this you consist of—all folded in together with the you of this moment? Just as something enables the transformation of a shy six year-old into a fierce elderly man at sixty, even as the old contours of his six year-old face remain unchanged in his sixty year-old face?

Is it, then, another you that powers your reading of this story? A you that is usually hidden, in meetings of bodies, behind the empirical representation of the you that is your face, now gently starting to reveal itself as you begin to accept the *you* of a story like this, though it is, of course, not yet completely clear, exactly how and where they all fold in together, this other you who both is, and is not you. Let us leave it at that for now. Can you sense it now, if only faintly? How you mistook me? How the object of your silent retorts was actually yet another you? And so there you are, necessarily spread across that vast distance between you yourself and the you that is my *you*! It is impossible, here, to fasten you to either one of these

를 고스란히 나 자신으로 품고 싶다. 원심력의 욕구를 가지고 나로부터 떨어져 나가려는 한 의식의 반대편으로 일종의 구심력을 작용시키며, 내가 팽팽하게 둥근 하나의 폭으로 열리도록.

그런데 얼핏, 의혹이 든다. 내 주장이야 어떻든, 정말 내가 여기서 이인성 그 자신으로 표출되고 있을까? 조금 전, 사설이 거창하게 번진 것부터가 미심쩍다. 혹시 나는, 이 소설을 쓰는 이인성과는 다른, 다만 소설 속의 이름이 이인성일 뿐인 다른 이야기꾼이 아닌가? 적어도 '나는 이 소설의 작가 이인성이다'고 했을 때의 나는 작가라는 특정한 역할 속의 이인성이라는 역할을 맡은, 작가로서의 '나' 자체를 가장한 별개의 '나'라는……. 그렇다면 '그 자신'이니 '자체'니 하는 표현보다는……, 에, 그러니까…….

일단 멈추겠다. 자꾸 따져나가다 보니 인사 하나가 너무 게걸스럽다. 더구나 이 자리에서는 당신이 더 중요한 주인공인데도. 그러니까 이 순간은 그냥, 애초의 목적을 위해 일상적인 말투로 간략히 인사를 대신하는 것이 어떨지. "전, 이인성이라고 합니다. 감히 내놓고 말씀드리기가 좀 뭐하지만, 소설갑니다. 워낙 평범하게 살

sides. Not when I am calling upon these two yous as one.

Therefore, if we are to hope that this new necessity might steep its way into the reading action of the eyes themselves, you must, from now on, if only when skipping those spaces between lines, momentarily (and if needs be, consciously) stop the progress of your gaze.

Come to think of it, I've already made quite a bit of progress with this story on the subject of you (not to mention the unavoidable subject of me, and the inextricable relationship between us). Just as the title of this story in the table of contents must have seemed an open hint, back when you first picked up this collection of stories titled "Endlessly Low Breaths." It occurs to me that an official greeting is long overdue. With my sincerest apologies for this oversight, here, better late than never, is my welcome:

—Dearest Reader, Hello. I am the author of this story, Yi In-seong. And now, as I write this story, a story not just on any subject but on you, I...

Even in this moment, as I write this greeting, I am suddenly swept up by the notion that I would like

아와서 특별히 소개드릴 만한 건 없고, 그저 나름대로
세상에 나와 뭘 할 수 있을까 고민하다가 이렇게 소설
가가 되었지요. 삼십 대니까 팔팔한 나인데, 게으른 데
다가 밥벌이도 해야겠고 하다 보니, 소설다운 소설도
제대로 못 쓰고……. 아, 지금 쓰는 거요? 이건 소설가
인 제가 독자인 당신께 직접 말을 트는 척하는 그런 건
데요, 쓰다 보니 별로 신통해 보이지 않고, 원……" 하
고. 이게 너무 밋밋한 맛이라면, 무대 위의 스타를 흉내
내볼까. "안, 녕, 하세요?! 조용필, 아니, 이인성입다! 오
늘의 쇼, 아니, 소설은……" 어이쿠, 이건 영 못 해먹겠
다. 내게는 전혀 어울리지가 않는다. 그렇지만 말이 나
온 김에 연상되는 건데, 이 상황의 나는 무대 위의 가수
나 배우와 흡사하다. 그들의 신상명세보다는 노래나 연
기가 참으로 중요하며, 그나마 일방적으로 자신은 소개
했지만 당신을 소개받을 길이 없다는 점에서. 그래도
객석의 당신이야 어렴풋이나마 보이고 간혹 실존의 증
거인 헛기침도 들리지만, 책 읽는 당신은 있는지 없는
지조차 정확히 알 수 없으니, 이 처지가 더 비극적으로
(?) 과장될 여지가 많다. 때때로 가슴을 두드리는 느낌
—아무도 없는 길 위에서, 하늘의 눈 아래 혼자 벌이는

for you to attend to the mode of this greeting itself. True, I am the teller of this story, but it is not as if I have a different name in this story as its teller. Within this text, too, I aim to be the same entity as the Yi In-seong whose name is printed on the cover of this book. This may sound strange, but it is a very important point. Right now, I, as I have up to now and plan to be, overall, and from now on, am striving to keep myself from becoming the kind of storyteller who exists only in the story itself.

This statement is not to be confused with your relationship with yet another you, as already discussed on the subject of you. Of course, the act of enforcing such regulations on the subject of you has also left me feeling the existence of another me. More than anything in the sensation of my hand moving the fountain pen across the page. Still, in the context of a story being written between me and yet another me, any considerations regarding other storytellers seem neither here nor there. It is as if those countless storytellers that go by names different from their authors, layers upon layers of them reaching a new density, have emerged through me to force a distance between me and yet another me, and are now approaching

어릿광대짓. 그런 날은 닥치는 대로 사람을 불러내고 쏘다니고 술을 퍼먹지만……, 이제 정색을 하자면, 진정 당신은 누구인가?

당신은 진정 누구인가? 독자로서 이 소설 앞에 이르기까지, 당신의 나이만큼 살아온 그 전체로서의 당신은? 나는, 숨을 가득 들이쉬고 깃털을 곤두세우고 날개를 활짝 펴 무엇인가를 가득 품은 최대치의 당신을 그린다(끝내 얼굴은 그려지지 않는다). 그 당신의 이름이 밝혀지지 않는다고 남들 속에 숨어들며 대답을 피하지 말라(무작정 달려가 얼굴을 맞대고 싶은 열정을 애틋이 가라앉힌다). 아까와는 반대 태세로 오뉴월에 서리 내리게 뭔가에 사무친 처녀처럼 독기를 품고 말하는 바, 이 물음은 정면으로 당신에게 주어진 것이다. 미리 단서를 달아두었었지만, 당신의 대답을 들을 수 없다고 해서 반드시 대놓고 질문하지 말란 법은 없다. 아까의 경우와는 질문의 형태부터 다르다. 여기서 나는 위 질문을 절대격의 의문부호로 닫아, 어차피 외로운 나를 더 철저히 고립시키면서, 그 대신 그것을 당신의 살 깊숙이 당신에 대한 당신만의 물음으로 새겨넣겠다. 지금 당장 팔뚝을 펼쳐

with the faces of strangers, having inserted them-selves into that very space. This is why the act of writing a story always requires a certain decision to be made. What name should I give to that formless face, so familiar and yet so strange? Once named, it will leave me, become an independent agent and object. Whether this would, in fact, be a separation from me or a diffusion of me, having gained a sin-gular essence he will have become him. That said, today, I find that I wish to keep him intact inside of me, a part of myself. My hope is to trigger, in re-sponse to the centrifugal force of his desire to separate himself from me, a kind of centripetal force within, opening me up in the form of a taut, round space.

But then, a flash of doubt. Whatever I myself might claim, am I really expressing myself here as Yi In-seong himself? My suspicions go back a few moments, when the prose began to bleed into the realm of the bombastic. Is it possible that I am Yi In-seong, the storyteller within this story, separate from the Yi In-seong who is actually writing this story? At the very least, the *I* that claimed, "I am Yi In-seong, the author of this story," was claiming, too, to be the *I* as the author writ large, the *I* as

보라. 거기 이미 새겨져 있지 않은가? 보이지 않는, 그러나 진하게 느껴지는 문신이. 그 허구의 문신을 바라보며, 당신은 홀로 내밀하게 발음해야 한다. "나는 진정 누구인가?"

여기야말로, 당신이 자발적으로 당신 스스로를 향해 많은 시간을 쏟아야 할 곳이 아닐까?

당신만의 시간 이편에서, 내 몫으로 머릿속에 떠올라 혼탁하게 뒤척였던 꿈그림자 : 누구일까, 한 아이가 희디흰 햇살의 운동장을 가로지르고 있었다. 주위에는 아무도 아무것도 없고, 오로지 빛의 공간만이 아득히 확대되는 거기서, 빛 위를 걸을 수 있는 신발인 양 작은 그림자만을 신은 채. 한없는 걸음. 그러다가 홀연히, 아이는 빛 속으로 사라졌다.

이제, 과감히 한 단절의 단락을 앞에다 세워놓고 나서, 다시금 어떻게 「당신에 대해서」란 제목을 위해 당신에게로 다가갈까? 아마도 그 때문이었겠지만, 조금 전 당신의 정체에 대한 물음을 전적으로 당신에게 몰아붙인 후 햇살과 아이의 몽상마저 사라졌을 때, 한 유혹의

distinct entity assuming the appearance of self, the Yi In-seong who has taken on the specific role of the writer... Which means, perhaps, that rather than terms like *self*... ah, that is...

I'll stop, for now. Following this train of thought has turned what was supposed to be a straightforward greeting into something far too gluttonous. Besides, you are the more important protagonist here. So for now, in this moment, how about a simple greeting in a casual tone instead, more in keeping with the original goal. "My name is Yi In-seong. I'm a writer, though it's a bit embarrassing to just say it like that. I've led a pretty ordinary life, so I haven't really got much to say by way of introduction; it's more that after wondering for a while about what I should do with my time in this world, I ended up becoming a writer. I'm in my thirties now, so I'm in my prime, but I'm a bit lazy and still have to make ends meet, so I haven't quite got around to writing the kind of story that makes you go, well, now *that's* a story... Ah, what am I working on right now? Well, this is something where the writer, me, pretends to speak directly to the reader, you, but now that I've made some progress I'm not so sure about this anymore..." Or, if this strikes

손길이 내 속의 어느 곳에서 내 속의 다른 곳으로 뻗쳐 나왔었다(당신 속에 침잠해 있는 동안, 당신도 어떤 손길을 만났는가?). 누군가—또 하나의 나였을까, 내 속에 들어와 있던 엄연한 남이었을까—가 낮게 속삭여댄 것이다(당신이 만난 손길은 얼마나 거칠고 얼마나 부드러웠는가?). "앞의 그 태도는 아무래도 무책임하다고 판단되지 않아? 지나치게 방관자적으로 한발 물러서는. 더 적극적일 수는 없을까? 그런 뜻에서, 너의 '당신'을 이쪽에서 능동적으로 추출해내면 어떨까? 예컨대 이 책의 속성에 비추어 그 독자들을 분석해봐. 소설집도 가지각색이니까, 그중에서 이런 유의 소설집을 구입하거나 뒤적일 만한 사람들을. 이 책을 펴낸 출판사의 평판, 광고 방식, 이런 유의 책을 갖다놓는 서적과 고객 성향, 저널리즘의 소개, 또, 비평가들의 관점 등등, 그런 것들을 종합해서 말야. 그러면 그들이 속한 사회적 계층이라든가 경제적 능력, 지적 수준 따위를 어느 정도 객관적으로 추적할 수 있을 거 같은데. 거기다가 별로 알려지지도 않은 너란 작자의 소설까지 읽어가고 있다 칠 때, 문학에 대한 관심이랄지 취향, 혹은 의무감이라도 지니고 있을 게 거의 틀림없고 말이야. 그런 특성들을 모아 재구성해 보면

you as too plain, maybe creating the impression of an onstage rock star would be better? "How you doin' tonight?! I am Jo! Yong! Pil! I mean, I am Yi! In! Seong! Tonight's show, I mean, story..." Oh, boy. That just won't do. It doesn't suit me at all. But while we're on the subject, it does occur to me that the position I'm in is so very different from that of a singer or an onstage actor. At least, in the sense that their singing and acting is far more important than any of their personal details, and that, while they may introduce themselves, there's no way for them to receive your introduction in turn. Then again, they still can make out the faint sight of you in your seat, they can still hear the occasional cough, that proof of the audience's existence, whereas there is no way at all of knowing whether or not the you reading this book is even there; indeed, there is a great deal of room for this latter condition to be exaggerated into the downright tragic. That feeling that occasionally knocks against the chest—that this is all just nonsense in an empty street, performed alone under the gaze of the heavens. On days like that, though, it's best to just call up whoever comes to mind and go out on the town, drown it all in drinks... but anyway, now, let's

그런대로 구체성을 띠지 않겠어? 그래서 하나의 전형을 만들어내는 거야. 그땐 훨씬 적절하고도 강력한 대응 문맥을 구할 수 있겠지." 적극적, 능동적, 속성, 분석, 사회, 객관적, 재구성, 구체성, 전형, 대응……. 그 낮은 목소리는 그다지 싫지 않게 거칠었고, 또 그 나름의 단단한 사랑의 표현임에 틀림없었다. 그래서 외로운 액체성의 독기를 품고 있던 내 가슴속의 여성—그녀는 또 누구?—이 하마터면 그 남성적 에로티즘에 매혹되어 몸을 풀어버릴 뻔했다. 아니, 그때 눈꺼풀을 덮고 새어 내보내던 가느다란 신음을 미리 기록해두지는 않았지만, 그녀는 이미 그의 앞에 몸을 눕히고 있었다. 그러나 그 이상은 아니었다. 그의 애무는 그녀의 성감대를 찾아내지 못했다. 그의 손길은 오히려 그녀의 살갗을 차갑게 굳힐 뿐이었다. 아마도 그녀는 그 어휘 체계의 에로티즘이 껴안을 상대는 아니었던 모양이다. 지금, 그녀는 내 가슴의 컴컴한 어둠 속에서 홀로 무릎을 세우고 앉아 하염없이 가슴 바닥을 두드리고 있다.

나는 앞의 방식을 제안해준 그 누군가의 굳센 순정을 의심치는 않는다. 내 가슴에 울린 그의 목소리의 색채가 그것을 전해주었으니까. 이 비실증적 증거를 기꺼이

get serious: Who are you, really?

Who are you, really? The you before you came to this story as a reader, the you that encompasses all the lived years of your current age? Filling my lungs with air, all my feathers standing up on end, opening my wings wide, I imagine the very best you I can, a you being filled to the brim with... something (though I still can't picture your face). Don't use the fact that your name will never be exposed as an excuse to hide amongst others that may or may not be reading this and avoid answering the question (fondly, I try and settle the desire to blindly race to where you might be, to try and see you face to face). In stark contrast to before, in the words of a malicious young woman with some deep grudge, in a tone cold enough to bring frost in June: this question is for you, given in a straightforward tone. True, certain conditions have already been laid out, but there's no rule saying that just because I can't hear your answer, I also can't ask you a plain question. Besides, the actual type of question I'm asking here is different from before. So, now, having closed the above query with a question mark, and fully isolating my already lonely self even further, I

용인하는 내 성적 상상력은 그러나 그와 나를 결합시켜 주지 못했다. 찬찬히 따져보면, 이 어긋남은 당연하다. 실은, 애당초 그런 상상력의 차원에 성급히 몸을 내맡긴 것부터가 잘못이었다. 나는 혼돈에 빠졌었음이 자명하다. 그 순간의 외로움에 마비되어. 그를 그야말로 그의 방식으로 보지 않고, 내 방식으로 그의 문맥 속에서 정당한 한 인간으로서의 참모습 그것만을 끌어안으려 했던 까닭에. 하지만 그와 나의 결합은 서로 다른 무기를 들고 같은 전선에 나란히 선 전우애의 상상력 속에서나 이루어질 성질이었던 것이다. 거기서 그와 나는 당신의 삶의 공간 속에 근본적으로 의미 좌표를 달리하고 있는 어떤 표적을 겨냥하는 형국이랄까. 따라서 그의 의견을 수락한다는 것은, 지금까지 쓴 모든 것을 찢어버리고 또 다른 한 편의 소설을 새로 시작해야 함을 뜻한다. 당신과 내 이야기꾼이 고유명사로서의 이름을 나눠 갖고. 그런데 아니다. 내가 여기서 실천하고자 하는 행위는, 소설이라는 형태를 매개로 최대한 가까이 접근하여 그 최소한의 간격만을 유지한 채, 즉 소설 쓰기와 소설 읽기라는 상황으로 우리—우리? 오, 우리!—를 수렴시켜, 모든 당신을 '당신'에게, 모든 나를 '나'에게

will etch it instead deep into your flesh: a question about you, asked of you alone. Look down at your arm right now. Isn't it etched in there? A tattoo, impossible to see but easy to feel, its thickness. Gazing upon that imaginary tattoo, you must say the words, articulating the syllables in private: "Who am I, really?"

And this, in truth, is where you really ought to voluntarily spend some real time on yourself, isn't it?

For my part, here on this side of your time alone, there is the issue of that image, the murky dream shadow of me tossing and turning: who can it be, this child in the white sunlight, crossing the schoolyard. There is nothing and no one around, just a place of expanding light and space, a pair of small shadows worn on the feet like shoes that can walk on light. Endless steps. And then suddenly, the child disappears into the light.

So, now that I've boldly committed to a line break and a new paragraph, how am I to approach you to further serve the title of this story, "On You"? This is probably why, even when the dream of the

끊임없이 되돌리며 되씹게 하는 일이다(그러므로 이미 지나왔지만, 내가 그의 목소리를 재현하고 잘못 발 디뎠던 그와의 에로티즘을 묘사했던 곳에서도, 당신은 그 환상에 동화되어 같이 나뒹굴지 않았어야만 했다). 그 무수한 당신이, 그 무수한 내가 누구이건 간에. 자기 자신으로부터 아주 작게, 그러나 본질적인 변모의 가능성을 향하여. 마침내 그 언젠가, 무한히 서로를 만나기 위해. 그리하여 그때 그곳에서는, 우리―이 어휘의 존재 방식부터 떠올려야겠지만―의 아름다운 성적 상상력을 완성시키기 위해.

"이봐요, 이인성 씨! 여길 그냥 지나칠 수가 없는데," 하고, 불쑥, 이번엔 내 몸 밖 어디서의 누군가가 글길을 막는다. "잠깐 이야기 좀 합시다. 당신 나름의 작가적 순수성이랄지 성실성이랄지 하는 건 인정한다 처도, 정작 그 문학적 태도엔 심각한 회의가 가는데, 좀 따져봐야만 되겠소. 우선 단도직입적으로 물어, 도대체 이 소설을 가지고 뭘 바라는 거요?" 내가 당신을 '당신'이라 부르듯 누군가가 나를 '당신'이라 지칭하는 게 몹시 기꺼워, 나는 흥분에 휩싸이며 주위를 둘러본다. 그것은 지금 이 소설을 쓰고 있는 방 안의 책장에 꽂힌 어떤 책들이 합쳐져 만들어낸 음성이다. "방금 말씀드리지 않았

child and the light disappeared, right after I blind-sided you into accepting full responsibility for that earlier question about your identity, a hand of temptation grew from some spot inside me and stretched out towards some other spot in me. (Did you, too, meet with any hands while you were withdrawn into yourself)? Someone—was it another me, or was it some undeniable other already inside me—spoke to me in a low whisper (how rough was the hand you met? how soft?). "Don't you think this attitude you've adopted is a bit irresponsible, when all is said and done? Stepping back so completely to the sidelines is a bit much. How about a little more involvement? How about a little active investigation into this *you* of yours, here on this end of things? For example, you could try using the attributes of this text to an-alyze its readers. There are all kinds of story col-lections, after all, so who would be the type of person who buys or flips through this kind of col-lection in particular? I mean, try synthesizing the reputation of this book's publisher and their mar-keting strategies, the kind of store that sells a book like this and the tastes of its customers, the book reviews, the observations of various critics, so on and so forth. That way you might be able to start

던가요? 바로 당신을 원하는 거지요." 나도 그를 '당신'이라 부르며 대답한다(표면으로 불거져 나왔을 뿐, 그 또한 당신 중의 하나임에 틀림없다). "난 지금 그렇게 문학적으로 얼버무리는 소릴 들으려는 게 아니요." 그가 약간 성난 듯이 반발하며 말을 잇는다. "이게 우리의 삶에 실제적으로 무엇을 기여하느냐, 알고 싶은 거지." 이 대화를 회피할 수는 없으니, 아무래도 당신에 대한 직접적인 이야기는 잠시 미뤄둬야겠다. 그러나 여기서, 당신도 방관자로 한발 물러서서는 안 된다. 당신은 그가 아니고 내가 아니며, 따라서 여전히 당신으로 참여해야 한다. 이제 내가 말하겠다. "난 이 소설의 문맥 속에서 대답했을 뿐 결코 얼버무린 게 아닙니다. 헌데 당신은 소설가인 나에게, 그것도 소설 속에서, 명료한 의식의 부분, 논리의 부분만을 떼어내라고 요구하고 있습니다. 그게 내게는 몹시 거북살스럽다는 걸 이해하시겠지요? 그러니까 부호 하나 빼놓지 않은 이 소설 전체가 그 자체로 내 대답이라 말하는 게 내 식으로 타당한 대응이겠지만, 일단 당신 소리에 귀를 기울이고 말았으니, 한번 당신 뜻을 따라봅시다. 그럼, 당신들의 용어를 빌어 대꾸해볼까요? 이런 소설을 쓰는 건 바로 이 소설을 읽는 독자

getting an objective sense of their social class or earning power, their intellectual standing. Add to that the fact that you're not a particularly famous author, and the fact that their reading your story tells you that they definitely have a deep interest in literature, or unusual taste, or, at the very least, some sense of duty driving them. Don't you think if you took these characteristics and reconstituted them, you'd reach a kind of specificity? And with that you could create a singular model, of sorts. Then you'd be able to come up with a much more powerful, apt, and responsive semantic vein." Involvement, active investigation, attributes, analysis, objectivity, reconstitution, specificity, model, responsivity... The roughness of this low voice was not altogether unpleasant, and there was no doubt that this was, in its way, an expression of love. Indeed, the malicious (a malice born of loneliness) woman in my heart—and who, now, might she be—was nearly undone by the masculine eroticism of it all. No, it's not as if I recorded the thin moans that leaked out of her, but, eyes closed, she has already laid herself down before him. But there was no more beyond that. His caresses failed to find her erogenous zones. Rather, his hands left her skin

로서의 당신을 해방시키기 위해섭니다, 라고." 그 : "해
방? 이게 어떤 식으로 인간 해방과 관련을 맺는지 말해
보겠소?" 나 : "대개가 다 그렇지만, 이 소설도 삶의 여러
양상 중 어떤 하나에 초점을 맞추고 있다는 걸 미리 염
두에 두어줬으면 좋겠군요. 여기선, 내 소설을 읽는 독
자 자신이 스스로 느끼고 스스로 꿈꾸고 스스로 반성,
비판하는 정신적 실천의 영역에서지요." 당신(계속 읽고
있을 뿐이므로 이 대화에 직접 끼어들 수는 없어도, 독립된 말 자
리만은 갖추어 두어야겠기에) : "

                                    " 그 : "구체적인 현실이 삭
제된 소설을 통해 정신적 실천이 행해진다는 건 공허한
관념론으로 들리는데……." 나 : "가볍게 반문해봅시다.
밥 벌어먹기 위해 몸을 움직여 일하는 것만이 구체적인
현실이고, 소설을 읽고 몽상하고 성찰하는 건 그렇지
않다는 건가요? 그거야말로 독단적 관념론이 아닐까
요? 지금 나는 독자의 책읽기라는 '구체적인 현실'을 겨
냥하고 있는 겁니다." 그 : "내가 지적하는 건 독자의 개
체적 현실이 아니라, 그들이 모두 함께 어우러져 사는
사회적 현실이요. 인간 해방이란 명제가 개인의 차원에
머물러서도 안 되고 머무를 수도 없는 건데……, 역사

colder and harder than before. It would seem that the eroticism of his language did not render him, for her, into a viable partner for physical embrace. Right now, she sits alone in the darkness inside me, her knees clasped to her chest, pounding the floor of my heart over and over again.

I have no suspicions about the pure intentions of whomever it was that suggested the methods outlined above. This is because the color of his voice, as it rang through my heart, clearly communicated those same intentions. Even as my sexual imagination readily admitted this dross as so-called evidence, it still failed to unite him with me. Indeed, a thorough accounting reveals this mismatch to be only natural. In truth, my first mistake was to surrender myself so quickly to the imaginary dimension. It is self-evident that I fell into a state of confusion. Paralyzed by the loneliness of the moment. Rather than see him through his own lens, I struggled to embrace only his true character as a just human being, all from within the realm of his language. All when what was actually required for our union was an imagination of comradery, of two men standing abreast on the front lines, each holding his own weapon. We might say that this is a sit-

의 진보를 논할 때, 거기서 궁극적으로 바뀌어야 할 것은 인간들이 함께 실재하는 이 사회, 이 세계일 테니까 하는 소리요. 그에 비추어보자면 당신은, 개인의 구원이 해방의 완수인 양, 또 문학과 독서의 혁신이 곧 세계의 혁신인 양 착각하는, 뭐랄까, 일종의 정태적 개인주의, 자폐적 문학주의 같은 데 빠져 있는 거 아니겠소?"

나 : "어떤 명제가 헛된 구호로 전락하지 않기 위해선, 그 명제의 실행 조건들이 문자 그대로 구체적으로 검토되지 않으면 안 됩니다. 그런 의미에서, 아주 상식적이지만 그래서 오히려 자주 무시되는 사실부터 이야길 시작하겠는데요, 그건 개인이 사회적 조건 속에 실존하는 만큼 사회는 개인 실존들에 근거하고 있고, 동시적이며 불가분리의 관계인 이 둘은 함께 얽혀 움직이고 있다는 겁니다. 그러니까 세계가 바뀐다고 할 때, 바뀌는 것은 표면적인 사회 구조만이 아닙니다. 사회가 바뀐다는 것은 곧바로 인간이 바뀐다는 것을 뜻합니다. 인간의 정신과 삶의 양상 일체가 변화하는 거지요. 올바른 인간 해방 운동은, 따라서 세계 내 삶을 구성하는 모든 영역들이 더불어 전진해나갈 때 완수될 수 있는 게 아닐까요? 여기서 나는, 문학도 인간의 정신 활동과 관련하여,

uation where he and I are aiming at targets with fundamentally different coordinates of meaning within the space of your life. It follows, then, that accepting his opinion requires everything written up to this point to be ripped up, and that I would need to start an entirely new story from scratch. With you and my storyteller sharing a name, as befits a proper noun. But no, that's not it. The action I propose to undertake here is to use the form of the story as the medium of my approach, to get as close as possible, maintaining only the absolute minimal distance; that is, each of us being in the position of either writing a story, or reading a story, we—we? Ah, we!—may converge, endlessly turning every you back into *you*, and every me back into *me*. (We have already moved past this, I realize, but this is also why, back when I attempted to recreate his voice and describe the eroticism of encountering him, it was crucial for you to keep yourself apart from the unfolding fantasy). Regardless of who those innumerable you's, those innumerable I's, might actually be. Towards the possibility of a very small, but very essential, transformation of the self. And finally, someday, to meet one another. And so then, in that place, we— though we must first consider the method of being

그때 바뀌어야 할 중요한 과제로 판단하고 있습니다. 물론 문학적 의미의 사회화는 독자들이 그걸 통해 얻은 정신 능력을 집단적 생활 속에 발현시키는 데서 비롯됩니다만, 그 진실된 발현을 가능케 하려면, 우리는 현 체계의 근원적 뿌리부터, 즉 문학적 소통의 출발점부터, 그러니까 글쓰기와 글읽기의 과정에 개입되는 여러 국면부터 정면으로 문제 삼아야 된단 말입니다. 그 역동적이어야 한 일단 정지의 시간, 정서와 의식의 공간을. 당신이 이걸 단순하게 개인적—정태적이라 비난하는 건, 아마도 그 점을 간과한 성급한 정열 탓일 것 같은데요……." 당신 : "

　　　　　"그 : "위와 같이 미분화된 논리를 들이대는 것부터가 이미 사태를 정체화시키는, 운동으로부터의 국외자적 태도를 반증하는 것이오. 그걸 이해하지 못하겠다면, 이렇게 방향을 바꿔 이야기하겠소. 무엇보다도 당신 소설은, 당신의 그런 논리에도 불구하고, 그 의지와 방향성을 전혀 드러내지 않고 있잖소? 요컨대 운동적 성격을 띠려면 독자에 대한 당신의 전망을 명확히 제시하고 그걸 확산시키는 노력을 경주해야 되지 않겠소? 헌데 당신은 거꾸로 난삽한 요설 속으로 도피해

encapsulated by this vocabulary—might finally complete our beautiful sexual fantasy.

"Listen up, Mr. Yi In-seong! We can't just move on past this yet," this time, out of nowhere, a voice outside of my own body stops my writing in its tracks. "Hang on just a minute here, let's talk a bit. Even acknowledging your writerly purity, or sincerity, or whatever you want to call it, when it comes down to it I have my doubts about this literary attitude of yours, and I have some questions of my own. First of all, frankly speaking, what exactly are you trying to do with this story of yours? What do you want?" Rejoicing in hearing someone address me as *you*, exactly the way I've been addressing you as *you*, I am overcome with excitement and look all around me. The voice, I see, comes from the grand sum of all the books on all the bookshelves in this room where I am now writing. "Didn't I just explain? What I want is you." I answer, calling him *you* in turn (after all, while he may have come to the surface, there can be no question that he is yet another you). "I'm not interested in vague, literary equivocations." He sounds a little angry as he continues. "I want to know how this is actually going to contribute to our lives." Since I cannot avoid

들어가고 있소. 문학 전문가들이나 겨우 알까말까 한 파격을 즐기면서. 혼란한 일상 속에 들볶이는 민중일 일반 독자들은, 자신들에게 이미 내재된 역량을 분출시켜줄 명쾌한 해석과 실행을 바라고 있는데 말이오." 나 : "글쎄요……, 매우 미묘하긴 합니다만 여전히 당신 의견에 동의할 수는 없군요. 자칫 이 소설로서는 곁길인 이 대화가 너무 확대될 위험이 있으니까, 대범하고 짧게 이야기해보지요. 어쨌든 그 문제는 우리가 해방된 세계상·인간상으로서 어떤 전망을 확보하는가와 결부된 중요한 문제임에 틀림없는 것 같습니다. 책읽기로 한정시켜 이야기하자면, 작가가 일방적으로 제시해주는 바를 그대로 주입받는 독서는 내가 생각하는 독서의 이상형이 아닙니다. 해방된 사회의 해방된 독자는 최소한 주체적인 사고인이자 몽상가여야 합니다. 그때 작가란 단지 그 사고와 몽상의 계기를 그답게 주체적으로 마련해줄 뿐이지요. 거기서, 비로소 작가와 독자의 평등한 대화가 이루어지는 것 아닐까요? 미래의 작가는 우월한 윗자리에서 열등하고 수동적인 독자를 가르치는 자가 되어서는 안 되며, 그들 간의 자유와 평등이 그렇게 문학적 방식으로도 수행되어야 한다는 의미에서

this conversation, it seems I must postpone, for the moment, any more direct discussion on the subject of you. But keep in mind, you still mustn't retreat to the sidelines. You are not him, or me, and therefore you must continue to participate as you. Now, I'll go on. "I was simply answering in the vein of this story, not equivocating. You're the one asking me, a writer, and what's more, a writer within the story, to isolate one distinct part of my consciousness, the logical part. You understand, don't you, how uneasy that makes me? An appropriate response, to my mind, would be to say that this story itself, in its entirety, is my answer to your question. But since I find I am already engaged in this exchange with you, I will play along for the moment. How about, just to start off, I borrow your own words to answer your question. The reason I'm writing a story like this is to try and emancipate the reader of this story from themselves." Him: "Emancipation? Can you tell me how this is at all related to human emancipation?" Me: "You could say this about most stories, but I'd appreciate it if you'd keep in mind that this story, too, is focused on one of the countless different facets that make up our lives. Here, the reader reading my story spontane-

요. 내 소설이 취하는 파격은, 그 바람을 지금 여기로 바싹 끌어당기려는 시도와 현실과의 갈등에서 빚어지는 결과겠지요. 그러니까 바로 거기, 내 무의지적 의지와 무방향적 방향성이 각인되어 있을 겁니다." 당신 : "

" 그 :

"이젠 아주 무정부주의자적인 면모까지 드러내는데, 본격적인 논쟁을 펼치고 싶은 생각이 용솟음치지만, 어차피 이게 당신 소설 속이니까, 그냥 다음 기회를 기다리도록 하겠소. 그 대신 한 마디만 덧붙여둡시다. 당신의 의도가 아무리 선량한 것이더라도, 그게 결과적으로 독자들을 절박한 현실에 동참시키는 작용으로 이어지지 않는다면, 썩은 세계에 안주하는 허위로 전락할 것이라고. 그걸 방지하려면 민중으로서의 독자의 실상과 만나야만 한다고." 나 : "입을 터버리고 말았으니 나 또한 차후의 논쟁을 마다할 생각은 없습니다. 여기선 나도 간단히 덧붙이고 끝내지요. 당신 또한 그 단단한 선입관의 틀을 벗어나 나의 이 노력과도 참으로 만나야 한다고. 전혀 별종의 짐승을 대하듯 '난해'란 학명을 붙이고 —기실 '난해'란 자신이 알고 있는 지적 체계를 벗어나 있다는 뜻 이상은 아닌데도—, 그렇게 선전된 내 소설

ously feels, spontaneously dreams, spontaneously regrets, all in an area of critical mental practice." You (as the reader, you are unable to participate directly in this dialogue, but designating a separate space for you feels somehow appropriate): "

" Him: "The notion that a specific reality, through a deleted text, can be carried out as mental practice sounds to me like empty theorizing..." Me: "Allow me a quick counter-question. Are you saying that working with one's body to earn a living is the only way of life that constitutes a specific reality, whereas reading novels and dreaming and reflecting does not? Isn't that a rather arbitrary theory itself? What I am engaging with here is the specific reality of the reader's reading experience." Him: "My concern isn't each reader's individual reality, but rather the social reality shared by all of them. Human emancipation is a proposition that must not, and, indeed, cannot, be limited to the scale of the individual. What I'm saying is that when we discuss the progress of history, that which most requires extreme change is this society, this world of shared human existence. Considering all this, it would appear that you are conflating the salvation of the individual with the object of

을 동물원의 구경거리로나 제쳐놓으려 하지 마십시오. 오늘의 독자들, 어쩌면 자기 문학관을 아집스럽게 고수하려는 전문가들보다 훨씬 유연할지 모르는 그들, 그들의 억압받는 미래에의 잠재력을 시급히 떠올려야 하겠기 때문입니다." 당신 : "

" 침묵.

의식을 곤두세웠던 힘겨움에, 내가 내 속에 풀어져 햇살의 운동장을 헤맨다. 햇살 때문에 아무것도 안 보인다. 캄캄한 햇살의 천지다. 이 빛의 어둠 속에 숨겨져, 한 아이가 울고 있다. 아이는 보이지 않고, 먼 울음만이 들린다…….

번번이 밀려드는 이 환영을 번번이 내 몫으로만 가두려 하지 말아야지. 그래, 그러니 물어야 해. 당신은 이 환영을 통해 무엇을 떠올리고 있는가?

나로 하여 또 당신 몫의 상념을 펼쳐보았을 당신은, 앞자리의 대화를 거치며 선명히 드러난 바, 단순한 단수 2인칭 대명사의 대상이 아니다. '당신'은 일종의 집합대명사다. 나는 '당신' 속에서 들끓는 복수를 본다. 하나

this emancipation, the reformation of literature and reading with a reformation of the world at large: aren't you, in other words, mired in a kind of static individualism, a near-autistic commitment to the world of letters?" Me: "To keep the original proposition from becoming no more than an empty catchphrase, the conditions of this implementation must necessarily include a consideration of the specific words themselves. To that end, I would like to begin with a point that may seem largely common sense and is, therefore, too often ignored: that as every bit of the individual exists within the conditions of society, society lives in the context of individual existence; simultaneous, inextricable, the two move together, intertwined. So when it is said that society is changing, what's actually changing is something more than just the apparent social structures. To say that society is changing is to say that humans themselves are changing. The human mind and the conditions of life are changing as one. As such, isn't it fair to say that any true human emancipation movement can only be rendered complete when all the different areas of life in this world make progress together? Here, I myself, believing literature to be an activity

의 중심 행위로 겹쳐진 복수. 그러므로 '당신' 속의 당신들은 책을 펼쳐 이 지면 위에 시선을 둔 하나의 자세로 집중되어 있되, 또 하나같이 각양각색인 조각들일 것이다. 그 당신들은 지금 어디서 어떤 모습으로 제각기 읽고 있을까? 가령, 당신은 앉아 있을까? 거실이나 다방의 소파에 등을 파묻고. 혹은 화장실 변기 위에서 무의식적으로 힘준 상체를 구부리고. 혹은 사무실이나 교실 책상에 팔꿈치를 의지해 손등으로 광대뼈를 고이고. 혹은 흔들리는 버스 창문에 비스듬히 기대어. 아니면, 당신은 누워 있을까? 하숙방이나 숙직실 맨온돌 위에서, 접어 세운 한쪽 무릎 위에 턱하니 다른 발을 얹은 채 두 손으로 어디선가 빌어온 이 책을 허공에 띄우고. 혹은 공원 잔디밭에 두 다리를 쭉 뻗고, 이 책으로 햇살을 가리며. 또 아니면, 당신은 엎드려 있을까? 텅 빈 연구실의 침대처럼 길고 평평한 열람대 위에서, 포개진 두 손등에 턱을 대고. 혹은 진짜 편한 침실의 침대에 어깨 위만 곤두세우고. 또 또 아니면, 당신은 서 있을까? 서점의 책장벽 한 모퉁이에 엉거주춤 기대어. 그것도 아니면, 당신은 걷고 있을까? 혼잡한 거리에서 (이런 소설의 경우엔 그러기가 쉽지도 않고 바람직하지도 않지만), 휘청휘청

of the human mind, consider it, too, to be an area that must also, crucially, change. Of course, the relevance of socializing literary meaning begins with the inherent opportunities for applying the expanded capacities of readers' minds as manifested in the context of their own social lives; but to make any such true manifestations possible, we must go to the roots, the very source of the current system, to the starting point of literary communication—we must, in other words, face and problematize the various conditions involved in the process of writing and reading. That necessarily dynamic, yet suspended moment, that space of sentiment and consciousness. For you to condemn this as individualistic or static is not only reductive, it seems to me the result of a passion that has led you to be hasty, and overlook the issue at hand..." You: "

" Him: "An insistence on the kind of undifferentiated logic displayed above not only serves to illuminate the situation at hand, it serves as counter evidence to any claim of an outsider attitude towards the emancipation movement itself. If you cannot understand that, then let me try a different approach. More than anything, isn't it true that your

행인들과 부딪치며. 또 그것도 아니면?……

　당신들의 생김새만큼 모조리 다를 그 자세나 동작들은, 그렇다면 그 이전의 또 얼만큼이나 다른 생활들로부터 연결되어 나온 것일까? 가령 앞의 모습들을 거슬러 올라가볼 때, 그 첫 그림은 일요일 오후의 지식인적 한가로움을 채우려고 이것저것 뒤지다가 이 책이 손에 잡혀서였을까? 한편, 그 옆은, 조용한 음악이 있는 다방에선 책이 읽고 싶어져요 하며 담배 피는 소녀적 취향에서? 줄줄이 엮어보자. 심각하게 우리 문학의 현황을 점검하려는 사명감으로 줄담배와 함께 읽어나가다가 갑자기 아랫배가 싸늘해져서? 어차피 쌓이고 쌓이는 타자용 서류뭉치를 피곤한 손길로 밀어놓고 상사의 눈치 틈을 타서 슬쩍? 강의 내용은 귀 밖을 맴돌고, 안 되는 연애는 괴롭고, '당신에 대해서'라니 이 속에 무슨 수가 없을까 싶어? 대학은 못 갔지만 의식만은 갖추어야 한다는 의지로 어디서든지 책을 놓지 않는 다부진 습관의 연장으로? 다른 필요 때문에 다른 글을 읽다가, 스며드는 궁상맞은 객지 기분을 잊기 위해? 이게 사는 꼴이냐, 비록 월급쟁이로 시달리지만 문화인다움의 긍지만은 잃고 싶지 않다고 그렇게나마 고즈넉한 시간을 얻게

story, despite this logic of yours, fails to demon-strate any of this professed will or direction? In short, if the goal is to emphasize the activistic character of a work, shouldn't you clearly state your view of your reader and do everything in your power to work towards proliferating it? Yet, in-stead, you are doing the opposite, seeking refuge in this flood of verbiage. Getting your fulfillment from the kind of shock tactics that might possibly interest a literary theoretician or critic (or not), but certainly no one else. All while the average reader, most likely a citizen subject to chaos of daily life, is hoping for a lucid interpretation and the possibility of practical application that might actually discharge his already inherent ability." Me: "I don't know... these certainly are delicate distinctions, but I find I still can't agree with you completely. In the context of this story this conversation is, ostensibly, a side-track of sorts, and there is a real risk here of over-magnification, so I will try to be bold and brief. Whatever the case may be, the fact remains that this problem is linked to the vital question of the prospect we are able to secure as emancipated figures of this world, figures of humanity. Let us limit the scope of this point to the issue of reading.

되면? 젊어 방황하고 있음을 순진하게 시위하고 싶어, 책 읽는 자기 모습을 공공연히 드러낼 만한 적당한 자리를 찾아? 웬일인지 열띤 친구들이 하나도 보이지 않는데 그럴 때의 그 무엇인가에 대해 혼자 버티고 위로받고 싶은 마음에서? 이만하면 잘 먹고 잘 사니까 머리라도 뭔가 이야깃거리를 채워놔야지 하는 심리로? 돈은 궁하지만 세상을 보려면 책을 읽어야 한다고 서점 순례를 몸으로 때우며? 새 책만 보면 공연히 궁금하고 들뜨는 성질에, 막 책방에서 사들고 나오며 우연히 펼쳤던 게 너무너무 재미있어서?……

그런데 이 순간, 막무가내로 가슴이 저려온다(그래서, 그러면 이 소설을 읽고 난 다음의 당신 모습은?─하고 묶일 질문이 뒤로 떨어져나간다). 당신들을 가능한 한 넓게 어지럽게 흩어놓으려 했지만 당신들이 흩어져 미치지 못하는 곳이 있음을, 또한 선명히 깨닫게 된 것이다. 나는, 막노동판의 인부가 도시락을 까먹고 철근더미에 기대어 이 소설을 읽으리라 도저히 상상할 수 없다. 캄캄한 갱도 속에서 곤죽이 되어 나온 광부나 재봉틀 앞에서 열다섯 시간을 기계로서 움직이며 파김치가 되는 처녀의 짧은 휴식과 나를 맺어본다는 건 터무니없다. 또 만약 문맹

The kind of reading in which the author unilaterally presents and the reader simply receives is not, to my mind, the ideal of reading itself. An emancipated reader in an emancipated society must, at the very least, be an independenet thinker and dreamer. And in this scenario, the only role of the writer is to provide, independently and in his own fashion, an opportunity for these thoughts and dreams to work. Indeed, isn't it in this precise locale that the writer and reader can, at last, engage in an exchange of equals? What I mean by this is that writers of the future must not be positioned far above, teaching down to inferior minds, passive readers beneath them; both the writer and the reader must carry out their freedom and equality in literary terms. What shock value my story has offered is most likely a result of the conflict between our current reality and my attempt to pull this hope into the here and now. And so my unintentional intentions and directionless directionality are carved therein." You: "

" Him: "Well, now you've revealed that you have a downright anarchistic quality to you, and this, in turn, has left me feeling a powerful urge to launch a full-scale argument against you,

자인 리어카 행상을 책과 연결시켜보려 한다면, 헌책을 근으로 달아 사서 헌책방에 넘기는 장사로밖에 가정해 볼 수 없다. 그렇게 지금, 그들은 모두 쓰기를 선택한 나와 읽기를 선택한 당신들의 밖에 있는 것이다. 그러니 이제, 뿔뿔이 널어놓은 당신들을 다시 하나됨에 모아들이려 해도, 그 주위에서 결코 '당신'으로 겹쳐지지 않을 그들이 외쳐대는 침묵에 휩싸여, 어찌 뼈저리지 않을 수 있겠는가. 이미 들린다, 당신도 들리는가, 귀울음처럼 흐르는 저 낮은 소리바람이. 그 신음과 한숨과 울분의 침묵이 묻는다. "넌 뭐냐?" 대답할 수 없음. "밥과 잠을 다오." 아무것도 줄 수 없음. 아까와 같은 대화라면 논리적으로 대응할 수 있으리라. 하지만 그 모든 것을 떠나, 그 모든 것 이전에, 맹목적으로 복받치는 이것은? 오, 푸르른 하늘님, 어찌하오리까?

……절벽 같은 탄식을 쏟아놓고도, 나는 이곳을 망연자실한 빈줄로 띄어놓아서는 안 된다고 버티는 한 가닥 의식의 응어리에, 만년필을 쥔 내 손에 안간힘을 모은다. 불모의 양심가책으로 그쳐서는 안 된다고. 가까스로 나는, '나는 왜 혁명가가 못 되는가'라는 자학적 질문 대신 '나는 소설가로서 무엇을 어떻게 할 것인가'라는

but, when all is said and done, this is still your story, so I'll just sit back and wait for my next chance. Let me just add one more thing. No matter how good your intentions, if they don't actually lead to bringing the reader closer to participating in this desperate reality of yours, your project will degenerate into no more than a falsehood, a settling for a rotten world. In order to prevent this, you must, as a member of the public, look on at the true reality of the reader." Me: "Well, as we've already begun, I, too, have no objection to continuing this discussion later. For now, I, too, will add just one more point: you, also, must cast off the mold of hardened prejudice and look on clearly at these efforts of mine, as well. Please refrain from simply labeling all of this as unintelligible (though it was marketed as such) as if you were dealing with some alien beast (despite the fact that *unintelligible* only means broken free of intellectual systems one already knows) and simply dismiss this novel as you might some spectacle at the zoo. After all, it is today's readers—individuals who may very possibly be a good deal more flexible than those so-called experts who cling to their own egoistic literary agendas—and the hidden potential of their repressed futures that constitute

생산적 질문에 작품으로 답해나가야 한다고, 스스로를 뒤집어 설득해본다. 하지만 여전히 뚫려 있는 그 순수 감정의 구멍을 어쩔 것인가. 아무래도 얼마간은, 그저 조용히 눈을 감고 있어야겠다.

당신은?

잠깐! 지금은 내 가슴 구멍을 메꾸기도 벅차지만, 그 곁에 도저히 죽일 수 없는 오기가 발동해서, 한 가지 당신에 대해 억지로라도 써놓아야겠다. 그래, 일부러 주의를 환기시키지 않는다고 어느덧 타성으로 돌아가, 이런 고통의 자리에서조차, 공백의 행간을 모르는 척 지나칠 참인가?

여기선 악쓰듯 다음 여백을 두 배로 더 넓혀놓겠다.

지금 당신은, 지금의 '지금'이라는 시간 단위 위에 있는 당신이 한정된 '당신'임을 깨닫고 있는가? 그러면 당신은, 그 언젠가의 '지금'엔 지금과 다른 당신이 되어 지금은 '당신'이 아닌 그 누군가들과도 함께 '당신'이기를 바라는가? 그래서 당신은, 그 언젠가로 가기 위해 무엇을 어떻게 쓸 것인가에 대한 하나의 응전인 이 소설에

my foremost concerns." You: "

                                " Silence.

Exhausted by my own bristling consciousness, I come undone inside myself and begin wandering the sunny schoolyard. The sunshine makes it impossible to see anything at all. It is a heaven and earth of sunshine, of pitch-brightness. Hidden somewhere within the darkness of this light, a child is crying. The child is not visible, only the sound of those faraway tears...

These images keep flooding back, time and time again—I shouldn't try and keep it to myself. Yes, I ought to ask. What does this vision call to your mind?

Having no doubt been prompted, by me, to consider countless thoughts of your own, you (as was clearly demonstrated in the preceding dialogue) are not the object of the simple singular second person. No, *you* are a kind of collective pronoun. I see your vengeance boiling over inside of *you*. A vengeance that will be combined with others' into one central act. Which means, then, that all the you's encompassed by *you* must be concentrating your gaze as

서 무엇을 어떻게 읽을 것인지에 대해 숙고해야만 하리라 믿는가?

너무 노골적으로 의도된 이 질문들을, 바로 그 점이 바람직하지 못하다는 이유로 취소하겠다. 단, 아주 인쇄를 삭제해버리지는 않는다는 조건하에.

다시 사이를 두고 뜸을 들였더니, 이번엔 매우 순진한 질문을 던지고 싶어진다. 당신은 왜 소설을 읽고 있는가, 왜? 움찔, 당황한 미소를 떠올릴 필요는 없다. 주위에 누가 있다 하더라도 이건 당신만이 읽고 있으니까, 마냥 자신에게 솔직하기만 하면 된다. 그런데도 이 질문이 난감한가? 이 질문의 폭이 너무 큰 까닭에? 그런 우려를 축소시키기 위해, 이 원초적 물음을 제한된 차원 속에 옮겨보자. 지금, 당신은 왜 다른 짓을 하지 않고 소설을 읽고 있는가? 왜 연극이나 영화나 텔레비전을 보지 않고, 왜 음악 감상이나 하지 않고, 왜 테니스를 치거나 조깅을 하거나 하다못해 골목 산책을 하지 않고, 왜 백화점 구경을 하지 않고, 왜 제 자식이나 조카와 그네를 타거나 장난감 조립을 하지 않고, 왜 친구들과 어울려 노닥거리지 않고, 왜 공부를 하지 않고, 밀린 사무

one on this page in this open book, an array of statues, each different from the last. Where, and how, are you all, each of you, reading this book right now? For example, are you sitting down? Maybe in a living room or a café, your back buried in some sofa? Or maybe you're on the toilet, your upper half bent over, straining unconsciously. Or in an office or classroom, your elbows on a desk, your hands against your cheekbones. Or, leaning sideways, body askew, against some vibrating bus window. Or, rather, are you maybe lying down? In a rented room or on the heated floor of a security guard's hut, one knee up with the other foot resting on it, both hands holding this book, borrowed from somewhere, up in the air above your face? Or, maybe you're in some grassy park with both legs stretched out, this book shading your face from the sun. Or, maybe, are you lying on your stomach? In some empty office or laboratory, stretched out on some table, long and smooth as a bed, your chin resting in your two hands? Or, maybe in a bedroom, on a truly comfortable bed, with only your head and shoulders upright. Or, or, if not that, then maybe you're standing? Leaning against a wall of books in some corner of some

를 보지 않고, 왜 집수리를 하지 않고, 화분을 돌보지 않고, 아내의 설거지를 돕지 않고, 왜 신문을 읽지 않고, 왜 사회학이나 역사학이나 철학 서적을 읽지 않고, 왜 시나 수필이나 평론을 읽지 않고……, 하필이면 소설을 읽고 있는가? 다른 게 귀찮아서, 또는 어쩌다가 그냥? 다른 게 다 귀찮은데 이건 왜 그나마 귀찮지 않나? 어쩌다가 그냥 붙든 게 어쩌다가 소설이냐? 무의식적으로라도, 어쨌든 당신은 소설에 다다라 있다. 속마음을 온통 뒤집어 훑어도 전혀 소설에 관심이 없고 뭔지조차 모르는 사람이 그럴 수 있을까? 다시 말해, 당신의 손길이 소설에 미친 것은 소설에 대한 어떤 최소한의 관념만은 잠재의식 속에 깊숙이 가라앉아 있음을 뜻하지 않을까? 막연히나마 소설이란 어떤 것이라는 판단과 거기서 대충 어떤 걸 구하리라는 기대로서.

여기서, 당신은, 그 자각을 실체화시켜보는 예로서, 이 소설을 처음 대하여 「당신에 대해서」라는 제목부터 읽기 시작했을 때 은연 중 예감해본 것을 상기해내 의식화시킬 수 있겠는가? 그때 당신은 교과서식으로 생각해, 어떤 제3의 가공의 인물을 '당신'으로 지칭하며, 그·그녀에 대한 애틋한 짝사랑의 고백을 하든가 어떤

bookstore. If not that either, maybe you're walking? Or maybe on a crowded street (though, in the case of this novel this would be neither easy nor advisable) swaying side to side and bumping into passersby. Or, if not that, either, maybe...?

Then how much of each of these poses, these actions—as different from one another as each of your faces must be—is a continuation of whatever lives that came before? Supposing we investigate these same poses, then maybe the first image I presented came from some Sunday afternoon, this book falling into your hand as you look here and there for something to fill your intellectual idle time? As for the next scene, perhaps a girlish urge to smoke a cigarette and read a book in some cafe with quiet music prompted it? Let's try cataloguing all of those poses, in turn. You have a sincere belief in the importance of knowing the current state of contemporary literature, you chain smoke as you read, driven by a sense of mission, until you suddenly feel a chill in your lower belly? You push aside that growing pile of papers with a tired hand and sneak in some reading here and there while your boss isn't looking? The class lecture just isn't sinking in, your love life isn't going well, you won-

비극적 사건을 함께 겪었던 상대로 설정하고 대화하듯 그걸 회상해보는 등의 소설을 염두에 두었었을까? 이미 내 다른 소설을 읽어보았거나 나에 대한 소리를 잠깐 들었던 바, 바로 이렇게 당신 자신의 상황을 그려주리라 확신했었을까? 그런 것들과는 전혀 상관치 않고, 아무 선입관도 없이 그저 읽히는 대로 읽을 태세였을까?

그러면 그 순간을 떠나 이제껏 자신의 시간을 이 소설의 시간에 걸쳐 놓아온 당신은, 드디어, 그 사이에 무엇을 어떻게 읽었는지도 깨닫겠는가? 최초의 예감이 충족되건 배반되건 초월되건, 그 두 다른 시간의 자장 속에서 다음 순간의 활자로 눈길을 지속해나가는 차례차례가 언제나 더욱…….

아, 당신이 꽤나 지겨워진 모양이다. 그렇게 몸을 비틀어대는 걸 보니. 하기야 멈출 듯 멈출 듯 이어온 이 눌변에 정신을 집중할 수 있는 시간적 길이로 봐서도 그럴 만하다. 또 마침, 어서 끝자리에 이르고 싶은 나로서도, 이미 지나온 이야기가 자칫 반복될까 걱정스러웠는데 적당히 잘라낼 수 있어 잘됐다. 그럼, 잠깐이나마, 불편하게 위축된 자세를 쭉 펴고 크게 기지개나 켜두자.

der if maybe "On You" might have some advice? The unbroken continuation of habitual studying, of your steadfast determination to make up for your lack of a college education by always developing your mind with constant reading? Because, reading some other book for some other reason, you wanted to forget that pitiable feeling of foreignness? A salaryman questioning if this is all there is, wanting to use what quiet moments you have in the pursuit of some form of culture? Searching, out of youthful rebellion manifesting in the naive desire for some sort of protest, for some public place to showcase yourself reading? Feeling, in the inexplicable absence of usually lively friends, the need for some comforting diversion to sustain yourself? Figuring, since you're doing pretty well for yourself, all in all, it might behoove you to fill your head with some worthwhile stories? Taking to heart the common wisdom that even if you're broke, all you need are books to see the world, and embarking on a bookstore pilgrimage? Suffering a condition of unnecessary curiosity and excitement that strikes each time you see a new book, and, upon opening it as you step out the store, finding yourself supremely diverted by what you find on the page...?

등이 뻐근하면, 두 손을 등 뒤로 뻗어 밀며 가슴과 배는 앞으로 힘껏 제끼고. 그렇지, 좌우로도 허리·어깨를 흔들면 좋다.

그러나 말이다, 약간의 여유를 가지고 당신과 편하게 어울리자마자, 번쩍 칼날을 세우는 초―의식이 개입해 들어온다. 이렇게 : 이 소설을 쓰는 나에겐 꽤 유용했던 방금 그 시간이 혹시 나에 의해 교묘히 유도된 것은 아닌가? 당신은 잘 읽고 있었는데, 내 지적 때문에 공연히 찌푸둥한 자세를 의식하게 되고, 내가 적은 대로 따라 해보고 있는 게 아닌가? 더 지나쳐서, 내 이야기에 맞춰 편하던 자세를 일부러 불편하게 고치기까지 한 건 아닌가? 그랬다면 당신은 내가 그토록 애써왔음에도 아직……? 아니, 침착하게 생각해볼 때, 오랫동안 소설을 읽는다는 일이 늘 그랬으니, 그 습관을 이 몇 페이지 안에서 뒤바꿔놓는다는 건 지나친 욕심일지 모른다. 게다가, 이젠 탁 터놓고 속과 겉을 완전히 뒤집어 밝히건대, 정말 곤혹스러운 점은 당신이 원래 너무도 자유스럽다는 사실에 있다(거기, 내 말 못 해온 고뇌가 있다). 소설 앞에서만은 언제나, 본질적으로. 글 속에 잠겨 단지 읽어주는 사람에게 이야기할 뿐인 내가 뭐라고 하든, 당신은

Yet, in this very moment, a stubborn ache settles in my heart (and with that, my next question for you—the image of you having just finished this story—has to be delayed). I have been forced to admit the unavoidable fact that despite my best efforts to spread the various you's across as broad a spectrum as possible, there are still places you cannot reach. I cannot bring myself to imagine, for example, a day laborer with his packed lunch, leaning against a heap of metal perusing this story. The very notion of an exhausted miner emerging from the dark of a deep mine shaft, or a young seamstress coming off of fifteen straight hours hunched over a sewing machine, either of them handing their precious free time to me—that would be nothing short of absurd. Trying to force a connection between this book and, for example, an illiterate rickshaw huckster, and the only likely image involves a pile of used books, tied together, being sold to a used book store. And so right now, in this moment, these people are all outside the parameters that contain the I that has chosen to write this, and all the you's that have chosen to read this. And so now, even were I to try and gather all these scattered you's back together into one, there still remains all those

완전히 당신 마음대로 읽을 수 있는 것이다. 내가 아무리 이렇게 읽으라고 한들, 당신이 저렇게 읽으면 도리가 없다. 나는 당신이 내 말의 직접적인 수신자이길 바라지만, 당신은 이미 '당신'이길 벗어나 나와 어떤 '당신'과의 관계를 관찰해보려는 제3자로 설 수도 있다. 그럼에도 조금 전의 당신이 만약 그저 멍청히 내가 지시하는 대로 몸놀림을 따라했다면, 그건 또 얼마나 역설적인 모순인가? 도대체 당신은 당신의 그런 자유를 스스로 깨우치고나 있었는가? 그리고 그 자유를 이때껏 충분히 행사해왔다고 자신하는가?

자, 당장 그 자유를 시험해볼 기회가 왔다. 곧 또 한 번 줄을 띌 참이니, 그냥 마구 뛰어넘든지 말든지 오로지 당신 뜻대로 해보라는 말이다. 의외의 전환이라고 꺼림칙해 할 이유는 없다. 이건 표면적으로만 모순되어 보이고 그 바탕에서는 처음과 같은 문맥이므로.

캄캄한 빛이냐 환한 어둠이냐, 나는 더듬어지지 않는 허공만 더듬는다. 저 아이를 이 드넓은 공간 어디서 찾을 수 있을까? 울음소리는 분명한데. 혹시 그 아이를 내가 품고 있는 것은 아닐까? 그 아이가 내 속에서 울고

who cannot ever be folded into *you*. Engulfed as we are in their silent protests, how can we not ache to our core? I can hear it already; can you? That low thrum of a sound, like a faint ringing in the ears? A question, those moans and sighs ask, a question in the silence of their pent-up rage: "Who do you think you are?" I have no answer. "Give me food and sleep." I can give them nothing. If this were a conversation like before, I might be able to respond with something logical. But this, aside from everything said before, before all of that— what is this surging up so blindly inside me? Oh, Lord in Heaven, what can be done?

...Even after releasing an ocean of moans, some small part of my consciousness cries out that I should not leave the devastated space of an empty line here, and so I grip my hand even tighter around my pen. This shouldn't conclude here with just some passing fit of conscience. I am trying to convince myself—albeit by only the narrowest of margins—that it is better for the question this story strives to answer to be productive (What can I as a writer actually do, and how can I do it?) rather than be a masochistic (Why is it that I am content here to be merely a writer? Why I am not a revolutionary?). But what to do

있는 것은 아닐까?

　나는 각설이처럼 타령으로 떠돌다가 빈손으로 되돌아온 것일까, 왠지 내 의식 속의 모든 것이 원점으로 되돌아와 있는 것만 같다. 그래서 한 가지 사실만이 분명하게 인식된다. 지금, 나는 쓰고 있다. 지금, 당신은 읽고 있다. 변함없는 현재. 나는, 지금 이 순간, '지금 이 순간'이라 쓰고 있는데, '쓰고 있는데'를 읽는 당신을, '당신을'을 쓰는 지금 이 순간에,……. 아니다, 나는 빈손으로 왔지만 빈 느낌으로는 돌아오지 않은 것 같다. 이상한, 이라기보다는, 자못 신비한 느낌이 든다. 지금, 나는 쓴다. 지금, 당신은 읽는다. 이때 나와 당신은 정말 동시적인가? 당신과 나는 다른 공간의 같은 시간 속에서 이 글을 주고받고 있는가? 현실적으로는 이렇다. 지금, 나는 쓴다. 지금 씌어지는 이 소설은 얼마 후 출판사에 넘겨져 편집되고 인쇄되어 책으로 제본되고 나서 책방을 거쳐 당신 손에 들어간다. 그때 당신은 읽을 것이다. 그러니까 내가 쓰고 있는 지금, 당신은 읽고 있지 않다. 지금 당신은 밥을 먹고 있거나 직장에서 사무를 보고 있거나 버스 안에서 졸고 있거나 화투를 치고 있거나 애인 팔

with this gaping hole of pure sentiment that still remains? There is nothing else to be done: for a little while, at least, I must close my eyes.

What about you?

But, wait! Though I am hard pressed at the moment just to stop up this hole in my heart, just besides that hole, an irrepressible defiance has also been aroused, a determination to put down just one more thought on the subject of you. Yes, without calling attention to the issue directly, it would be easy to return to habit and routine, to simply pass by—even in this place of pain—these empty line breaks as if we'd noticed nothing at all.

And now, here, like some sort of glutton, I will leave double the empty space.

Are you, right now, realizing that the you in the space above the right now of right now, that there is, in fact, a limited *you*? And if so, do you hope that in another "right now," someday when you have become a different you from right now, those others who are not *you* right now will have become the same *you* as you? And so, do you believe that you must now deliberate on what, exactly, to take

짱을 끼고 걷고 있거나 다른 책을 읽고 있거나 어쩌구저쩌구하고 있거나이다. 그런데 분명히, 다름 아닌 지금, 당신은 읽고 있다. 그렇지 않은가? 지금 막, '그렇지 않은가?'라고 당신은 읽지 않았는가? 하지만 당신이 이 소설을 읽고 있을 때, 내가 이걸 쓰고 있을 리 만무하다. 그때 나는 이미 썼다. 그러니까 당신이 읽고 있는 지금, 나는 늦잠을 자고 있거나 다른 돈벌이가 없을까 여기저기 기웃거리고 있거나 등산을 하고 있거나 술을 퍼마시고 있거나 부부싸움을 하고 있거나 다른 소설을 쓰고 있거나 어쩌구저쩌구하고 있거나이다. 그렇다면 나는 '나는 썼었다'라고 쓰거나 '당신은 읽을 것이다'라고 써야 할까? 그렇지 않다. 지금 나는 쓰고 있고, 지금 당신은 읽고 있기 때문에. 도대체 어떻게 된 일일까? 간격이 있는데 간격이 없다! 신비한 말의 모순이랄지, 현재가 과거로 불려가고 과거는 미래로 불려가 서로 엉겨 붙는다. 황홀한 반죽이다! 우리—문득 이 어휘의 실감이 스치는구나—가 마음살을 비비며 합쳐지는. 그러므로 글을 쓰고 읽는다는 건 애당초 그 결합의 첫걸음을 실천하는 일? 오, 이럴 수가……, 이렇듯 당신이 이미 나의 과거이자 미래이자 현재라니!…… 그래서 당신은 내가

from this story, and how to take it, from reading a story that is itself a response to the challenge of what to write and how to write it, in order to move closer to that very same someday?

These questions are perhaps too frank in their intentions. This is an inadvisable trait, and so I take them back. But only with the understanding that they are not to be deleted upon printing.

Another space, another moment's reflection, and now I find myself wanting to ask a rather artless question. Why are you reading a story at all? Why? No need to picture you flinching, your startled visage. It doesn't matter who might be nearby; you are the only one reading, so you need only to be honest with yourself. Does this question still have you at a loss? Is the breadth of it too broad? To minimize these concerns, let us narrow this question within some additional boundaries. Why, right now, are you reading a story instead of doing something else? Why not watch a play or a movie, why not listen to some music, why not play some tennis or go for a jog or, if nothing else, just take a stroll down an alleyway, why not windowshop at a department store, why not help your child or niece

숨 쉬는 공기 같은가? 등 뒤를 돌아본다. 당신은 없다. 몸을 되돌린다. 당신이 등 뒤에 있다. 그 보이지 않는 무수한 입자들로 떠도는 당신. 그러고 보니, 당신들끼리도 그렇다. 당신은 당신들이니까, 나의 이 지금으로부터 당신들은 시간과 공간의 거대한 좌표 위에 무수히 흩어진 점들이지만, 그러나 이 소설이 그 좌표 위의 어느 곳으로도 같은 형체로 다가가듯, 우리―뚜렷이 이 어휘를 새겨 지니고 싶구나―의 '지금' 속에서 그 간격을 지울 것이다. 그래서 어느 날 함께 말하게 될 터. 서로의 이 몹시도 작은 사랑에 대해서. 모래알 하나에 하나가 덧붙여지고 그 둘에 또 하나가 덧붙여지듯, 더디게 더디게, 하지만 또 어느 날 무겁고 거센 모래사태로 몰아치려고. 나와 당신은, 당신과 또 다른 당신은, 또 다른 당신과 나는, 그렇게, 철조망처럼 가로놓인 온갖 절차를, 검열을 광고를 소문을 기사를 비평을 거래를, 정치를 사회를 경제를 뛰어넘을 수 있으리라. 한없이 아득하지만 그래도 아무려나 갈 수 있으리라, 가야만 하리라. 그러니 그 미래의 현전인 이 순간만은 이 꿈에 기꺼이 도취해보자! 뒹굴자, 흙탕물에 맘껏 몸을 내던진 듯한 환상적인 전율로! 빛이 어둠인지 어둠이 빛인지,

or nephew put a toy together, why not hang out with your friends, why not study, why not work on that pile of office work, why not renovate your house, why not water a plant, why not help your wife do the dishes, why not read the paper, why not read a text on sociology, or history, or philosophy, why not read some poetry, or an essay, or a literary critique... why a story? Because everything else feels like a bother, or maybe just because? But if everything else feels like a bother, why doesn't this, too? Did the act or book or thing you just stumbled upon just happen to be a story? At any rate, even if the choice wasn't conscious, what you've arrived at to do right now is to read a story. Do you believe this is possible for someone without a single stitch of interest in reading stories, not a single hint of interest in some nook or cranny of your heart? In other words, doesn't the simple fact that your hand reached, at some point, for this story demonstrate the existence, at the very least, of a minimal, passing interest in stories themselves, buried somewhere deep in your subconscious? Just an idea, no matter how vague, of what a story is, and what might generally be gained from reading one?

내 어딘가의 여성이 내 어딘가의 남성과 섞여 아이를 낳았는가, 내 밖의 아이가 내 안에서 울고 있지 않으면 내 안의 아이가 내 밖에서 울고 있다…….

제대로 취해보지도 못했음에 틀림없을 당신이 왜 그리도 얼얼한 정신으로 비틀대는가? 이 말에 자존심이 할퀴어졌으면, 그만 돌아오라. 당신의 지금 여기로.

멀리, 당신의 웅얼거림이, 당신들의 웅성거림이 들린다. 물론 상상적으로, 그러나 너무도 사실적으로.

이제, 이것으로 한 매듭을 짓는 이 소설을 읽고 난 후의 당신은, 이전의 당신과 실오라기 간격만큼이나마 달라진 어떤 당신일까?

이제, 지금의 당신은 나의 다음 소설을 다시 읽으려 할까?

『한없이 낮은 숨결』, 문학과지성사, 1989

Is it possible for you, here, as a case study for the substantiation of self-awareness, to consciously think back on what presentiments you might have had, back when you first encountered this story and began reading the title, "On You?" Did you assume, back then, that this would be some by-the-book tale where a third imaginary party was addressed as *you*, and then what followed would be a touching confession of unrequited love for him or her, or, maybe that the story's conceit would involve a past tragedy shared with this *you* and the dialogue centered on reflections around it? Or, if you've already read another story of mine, or heard a little bit about me, did you have the sense that I would attempt, as I have right now, to describe your own situation? Or were you, with no such thoughts at all, no preconceived notions, simply ready for a story to read however it ended up reading?

Then, beyond that first moment, having spent this intervening time of yours overlapping with the time reading this story, have you, at last, come to understand what you have read along the way, and how you've come to understand it? Whether those first expectations have been fulfilled, or betrayed, or transcended, within the field of these two separate times, the movement of your eyes, with each moment, onto the next letter, and the next, one after the other, grows ever more...

Ah, it would seem you've become quite fed up. I see you, writhing in your seat. It's understandable, especially considering the sheer length of time spent concentrating on my ineloquent fits and starts, these countless false endings. And here, just in the nick of time, a welcome opportunity (for me, too, as I also would very much like to reach the coming conclusion) to address my concerns regarding further repetition of what has already been said so far and cut out what I can. So here, for just a moment, let us straighten our uncomfortably crooked postures and indulge in a nice long stretch. If your back aches, run your hands up and down your back and thrust your chest and stomach out with all your strength. That's it, move your head and shoulders from left to right, too.

But, you know, just as I try to settle in to this new and easy dynamic of ours, something sharp intrudes from my superconsciousness. Like so: is it possible that this moment we just shared, so helpful to me as I write this story, was actually a clever maneuver designed to serve my own ends? Is it possible that you were reading quite comfortably, and my observation is actually what made you aware of your own slouchy posture, and that this, in turn, is what led you to try following my written directions? Or, to go even further, is it possible that all this talk of mine made you uncomfortably adjust what was already a comfortable position? And if that was the case, does that then mean that you, despite all this effort you've put in so far to reading this story, are still...? No, when I consider this logically and calmly, it may be too much to ask that you reverse a habit you've built up over the entire length of this story in the span of just a few pages. Besides, now that we are opening up and bringing our darkest depths to light, I must say that what puzzles me most is your incredible freedom (and here lies the very anguish I've been unable to name). When it comes to stories, always, and fundamentally. No matter what I—from behind all these words—tell the person who deigns to read them, you are completely free to read this however you wish. No matter how much I insist that these words I have put down right be read a certain way, if you choose to read them a different way, there is nothing to be done. As much as I may want you to be a direct recipient of my words, you have already broken free your readerly limitations, and, indeed, may have adopted the stance of a third party observing the relationship I have been building with this other *you*. If, despite this, the you of some moments ago had simply and stupidly been following all my instructions to the letter, well, then, what a paradoxical contradiction this might be? Have you, at the very least, been coming to your own understanding of your freedom? And do you know that you have been taking full advantage of this same freedom up to this point?

Here, an opportunity to test this freedom at once. Soon I will skip another line, so what I'm saying here is that you are free to do whatever you like, to skip around here and there, or not, as you please. There's no reason to shy away from this at this unexpected turn of events. It only seems contradictory on the surface; this is, in fact, completely in keeping with where we started out.

The darkest light or the brightest darkness? I am groping at a void that cannot be felt. Where in this vast space can the child be found? The sound of his crying is clear. Is it possible that I have the child tucked away within me? Is it possible the child is crying inside me?

Have I just been wandering about, voicing my laments to the air like a rollicking homeless man only to return empty-handed? Maybe that's why every last part of my consciousness feels as though it's back at square one. Which leaves just one thing that I can still say with certainty. Right now, I am writing. Right now, you are reading. In this changeless present. Right now, in this moment, I am writing the words "right now in this moment," but the you who is reading "who is reading," in this moment that I am writing "writing"... No, I may have returned empty-handed, but I don't think I have returned feeling empty. I feel—not strange, exactly, but something almost mystical. Right now, I am writing. Right now, you are reading. In this moment are you and I truly in sync? Are we, in different places but at the same time, engaging in an exchange of these written words? Practically speaking, it goes like this. Right now, I am writing. After some time, this story that I am writing right now will be handed off to the publisher, where it will be

edited and printed and bound into a book, and after that, via a bookstore, it will end up in your
hands. Then, you will read it. So in this sense right
now, in the right now in which I am writing, you
are not reading. In this right now you are eating, or
working at the office, or drowsing on the bus, or
playing cards, or walking arm-in-arm with your
lover, or reading a different book, or doing this or
that, so on and so forth. But what's also undeniable
is that also, right now, you are reading. Isn't that
right? Didn't you just read the words, "Isn't that
right?" And yet, in the moment that you are reading
this story, I cannot be writing. In this moment, I
have already written it. So, in the right now in
which you are reading, I am either sleeping in, or
looking around for some other way to earn some
money, or hiking, or pouring drinks down my own
throat, or arguing with my wife, or writing a different story, or doing this or that, so on and so forth.
Then, does this mean that I should write that "I
have written," or that "you will read?" No, that's not
right. Because right now I am writing, and right
now you are reading. So how, then, does this
work? There is an interval, but there is no interval!
A contradiction in mystical terms, maybe. An en-

tangling of the present called into the past and the past called into the future. A rapturous mix! Where we—suddenly, a flash of feeling the actual meaning of this word choice—come together, one heart sliding against the other. Which means, perhaps, that the very acts of writing and reading are, fundamentally, first steps towards making this union a reality? Ah, can it possibly be... that you are already my past and my future and my present! Are you, then, like the very air I breathe? I look behind me. You're not there. I turn back around. You are behind me. You, roaming around as countless invisible particles. Come to think of it, this holds true even amongst all of you. Since you, here, are also the plural you, you are actually scattered, numberless across the vast coordinates of time and space, far from my own here and now. And yet, just as this story retains its form regardless of which of these points it approaches, we—I want to etch this word in here, this "we"—erase the interval within our joint *now*. So, someday, we will speak together. About this tiny love of these others. Like a single grain of sand joining another, and another joining those two, slowly, so slowly, only to rise up, one day, a powerful and frightening sandstorm. In this way I, and you, you and a different you, yet another you and I, will rise above the barbed wire fences of countless procedures, of inspections and advertisements and rumors and articles and critiques and negotiations, of politics and of society. It is all endlessly far away, still, but somehow we will still get there, we must get there. So in this moment, at least, let us give ourselves over and grow drunk on this dream! Let us roll about, throwing our bodies into these murky puddles, feeling the fantastic electricity running through us! Whether light is dark or dark is light, whether a woman somewhere inside me has joined with a man somewhere inside me and given birth to a child, either a child outside of me is crying inside me or a child inside of me is crying outside me...

Surely you are not drunk yet, so why are you swaying like that from side to side? Why is your mind so cloudy? If I've wounded your pride, well—still, come back. Back to your here and now.

In the distance, the murmuring hum of your speech—I can hear the murmur of all of you. An imaginary murmur, of course, but still, so real.

I wonder, are you now, having finished reading this story all the way to this end, a you somehow different—even by just the width of a single thread —from the you of before?

I wonder, will the you of this moment have any interest, now, in reading my next story?

Translated by Maya West

해설

Afterword

소통을 향한 전위

전소영 (문학평론가)

누군가의 의식이 활자에 담기면 그것은 텍스트가 된다. 또 다른 누군가는 그것을 읽음으로써 거기에 적힌 생각을 전달받는다. 이러한 과정을 우리는 흔히 독서라 부른다. 텍스트가 쓰인 시공간과 텍스트가 읽히는 시공간 사이에 필연적으로 거리나 시차(difference in time)가 존재하는 까닭에 독서는 이렇듯 대개 일 방향적 행위로 이해된다. 그러나 「당신에 대해서」(1985)에 따르면 이것은 '진짜 독서'라 하기 어렵다. 적어도 '소설'을 쓰거나 읽으려는 경우에는 그렇다. 정보를 실어 나르는 설명문과 달리 소설은, 끊임없이 서로의 존재를 의식하는 작가와 독자의 능동적인 상호작용을 통해서만 완성된다는 것

The Avant-garde as a Stepping Stone of Communication

Jeon So-yeong (literary critic)

The moment someone's consciousness is put into print, it becomes a text. And the moment a second someone takes in this resulting text, the original thoughts are transmitted to them. We call this latter process reading. Because there is necessarily a difference between the time and space of writing and the time and space of reading, the act of reading is most often understood to be singular in directional. And yet, according to Yi In-seong's short story "On You" (1985), this is not, in fact, true reading. At least, not when one seeks to write or read a story. The implication here, of course, is that there is a crucial difference between literature and

이다.

등단 이후 이인성은 이처럼 우리가 일반적인 것, 보편적인 것이라 알고 있는 패러다임에 지속적으로 의문을 제기해왔다. 문체나 형식의 차원에서 행해진 실험들은 그러한 내용을 좀 더 효과적으로 구현해내기 위한 방편이 되었다. 익숙해지거나 습관이 된 사물과 현상을 낯설게 그려내는 것, 그리하여 우리의 사유를 흔들어놓는 것. 이것은 이인성의 소설 세계가 지켜온 오래된 문법이다. 그의 작품에 한결같이 전위(avant-garde)라는 수식어가 따라붙는 이유도 여기에 있을 것이다.

「당신에 대해서」역시 그 연장선 위에 놓여 있다. 작품을 펼치는 순간 우리는 어김없이 독특한 내용과 형식을 맞닥뜨리게 된다. 소설은 뚜렷한 서사 대신 부정확하고 모호한 화자 '나'의 목소리로 가득 차 있다. 본래는 텍스트의 외부에 그것도 멀찌감치 존재해야 할 작가와 독자마저 이 소설에 이르러서는 시공간의 틈을 건너 마주선다.

예컨대 화자(narrator)인 '나'는 실제 작가와 구별되는 가상의 인물이어야 하지만 스스로를 작가 '이인성'이라 칭함으로써 허구와 현실의 경계를 허물어버린다. '나'는 또한 텍스트 바깥에 실체 없이 존재하기 마련인 독자의

any straightforward explanatory text that aims simply to transmit information; to Yi, the literary short story or novel is a form only made complete by the active back and forth conversation between writer and reader, each of whom, in turn, remains ever conscious of the other's existence.

Ever since his literary debut, Yi In-seong has made a habit of problematizing paradigms that the rest of us tend to consider both familiar and universal. In many ways, Yi's experimentation with style and form has been in the service of achieving these aims more effectively. To render strange once more those habits and objects so familiar to us; to destabilize our sense of self-possession: this mission has long made up the grammar of Yi In-seong's literary output. Which, in turn, is likely why critics and readers have so consistently used the term "avant-garde" to describe his prose.

"On You" is no exception to this rule. Like clockwork, the moment we open up to the first page we are confronted by the peculiar, in terms of both content and form. In the place of straightforward narration, the story overflows with the voice of a vague and inexact "I". Here, the writer and reader, traditionally seen as existing both outside the text

모습을 다양하게, 지속적으로 상상해냄으로써 복수의 독자(단수 '너'가 아닌 복수 '당신들')를 텍스트 안으로 초대한다. 이로써 작가인 '나'/이인성과 상상된 독자/실제 독자 사이는 좁혀지고 마침내 작가와 독자는 소설을 매개로 하는 하나의 공동체, 즉 '우리'가 된다. "나의 이 지금으로부터 당신들은 시간과 공간의 거대한 좌표 위에 무수히 흩어진 점들이지만, 그러나 이 소설이 그 좌표 위의 어느 곳으로도 같은 형체로 다가가듯, 우리—뚜렷이 이 어휘를 새겨 지니고 싶구나—의 '지금' 속에서 그 간격을 지울 것이다."

소설은 말한다. 결국 작가란 독자를 통해서만, 독자는 작가를 통해서만 자신을 확인할 수 있는 존재이다. 따라서 작가는 독자/당신을 끝끝내 끌어안아야 하며 독자는 텍스트의 내용과 길항하는 주체적인 사고를 세워 나가야 한다. 소설이란 곧 이들 사이의 영원한 대화다.

이 작품에는 이렇듯 부재하는 누군가를 그리워하며 그와 소통하고자 하는 열망이 담겨 있다. 이것은 암울한 1980년대를 견뎌야 했던 지식인의 것이어서 절실하고, 서글프다. 소통에 대한 갈망은 어쩌면 꿈이라기보다 인간의 본능에 가까울 것이다. 그러나 소설이 발표

and separate from one another, are brought together across time and space.

For example, though the narrating "I" is most often an imaginary entity separate from the writer, Yi wears away at the boundary between the real and the imagined by identifying himself directly as "author Yi In-seong." Yi's "I" then goes on to imagine, at some length, the diverse array of possible readers—readers bound to exist outside of the text. This move directly invites a plurality of readers (literally the plural "you" of many "you's" rather than the singular "you") to enter the text. Not only does this narrow the gap between the authorial I/Yi In-seong and the imaginary reader/the actual reader, it harnesses the story itself to mediate the transformation of writer and reader into one, into a *we*: "Since you, here, are also the plural you, you are actually scattered, numberless, across the vast coordinates of time and space, far from my own here and now; and yet, just as this story retains its form regardless of which of these points it approaches, we—I want to etch this word in here, we—erase the interval within our joint 'now.'"

The story speaks. Ultimately, the writer needs the reader, just as the reader needs the writer, in order

될 당시 한국 사회에서는 이 본능조차 용인되지 않았다. 군사 정권의 통제로 누구도 말이나 행동의 자유를 보장받을 수 없었으며 따라서 진정한 의미의 소통도 관계 맺기도 실현이 어려운 소망에 불과했다. 그 외로운 시대의 복판에서 이인성은 소설을 썼다. 「당신에 대해서」는 소설쓰기로나마 현실의 폐쇄성을 극복하고 소통을 향해 나아가고자 했던 의지의 산물이다. 그것은 지금까지도, 여전히 현재형으로 남아 있다. "이 마음이 당신에게 이해되기를. 지금 당장은 아니더라도 그 언젠가는."

to confirm his or her own selfhood. It follows, then, that the writer must enfold the reader/you in his embrace to the very end, and that the reader must pursue an independent train of thought that can contend with and against the unfolding text. After all, the story itself is, by definition, an endless conversation between these two.

This story is built on a deep desire for communication, a desire born of the longing for someone absent—a sorrow rendered all the more keen when we consider that it belongs to an intellectual of the 1980s, a particularly bleak period. True, one might argue that the thirst for communication is closer to human instinct than a dream. However, what is also true is that at the time of this story's publication, such an instinct would have been deemed completely unacceptable by Korean society writ large. The iron rule of the military dictatorship allowed no provisions for freedom of speech or action, effectively making true and open communication a difficult, and fairly ambitious goal. It was during this deeply lonely time that Yi In-seong penned this story. And so, in these terms, "On You" can rightly be considered no more or less than a product of sheer will: the will to overcome a claustrophobic reality through literature and move one step closer to true communication. This holds true even today. "I can only hope that you understand this stance. If not right now, then at least someday."

비평의 목소리

Critical Acclaim

이인성의 소설은 하나의 틀 속에 세상을 가두는 것 자체를 문제 삼는다. 그것은 세상의 무한한 분화와 복잡성을 하나로 통합하지도, 그대로 풀어놓지도 않는다. (…) 그것은 존재의 불안을 촉발한다. 그것은 그 불안을 끝끝내 감당하라고 다그친다. 세상 안에 튼튼하고 부드러운 집을 짓고 그 속에 누우려고 하는 우리는 당황하지 않을 수 없다. 그 당황감이 공격성에 뒷받침될 때 '난해'라는 딱지를 만든다.

정과리

The works of Yi In-seong seek to problematize the very notion of pouring the world into a single limited mold. To attempt to do so neither unifies nor untangles the world's infinite divisions and complications. [...] Rather, it serves to trigger our existential anxiety; it pushes us, insisting that we must manage this anxiety. As we seek to build sturdy, welcoming homes for ourselves in this same world, homes where we can finally rest, this insistence cannot help but disconcert us. And when this disconcerted state is backed by aggression, the label "unintelligible" gets trotted out.

Jeong Gwa-li

「당신에 대해서」를 쓰기 위해 작가는 매순간 독자이자 거울 속 자기 자신이기도 한 '당신'의 자리로 옮겨가 '당신'을 상상하고 다시 '나'의 자리로 돌아와야 하며 이러한 행위는 반복되어야 한다. 자리바꿈의 행위는 '나'를 중심으로 대상이 고정되는 인식 행위 자체를 다시 바라본다. 이를 통해 '당신'과 '나'를 타자화 하는 '그 당신' '그 나' 등이 가능한 것이다. 서술 내용에 괄호를 붙여 상반된 태도의 논평을 하면서 논평하는 행위 자체를 의식한다거나, '여기서(거기서)'처럼 여기 이 자리를 다른 자리에서 바라봄으로써 여기에 동화되지 않게끔 한다든가, '당신을 상상하면서(당신을 상상하는 나를 상상하면서)'에서처럼 대상을 사고하는 '나'라는 전제를 문제 삼음으로써 소설적 진실이 단정적으로 종결될 수 있는 것이 아님을 보여주고 있다.

정혜경

'소설 쓰기는 무엇이며 또 그 의의는 무엇이며 그것이 어째야 가능한가'라는 것. 그러기 위해 이인성이 맨 먼저 내세운 것, 묻는 것, 그것은 '소설 독자'의 분석에 있다. 그것은 협박조이기도 하고 또 달래기도 하면서, 추

In order to write "On You," the author shifts his position to that of his "you," a role that vacillates, moment to moment, between the reader and the self he sees in the mirror, all in order to better imagine "you." He does this only to return to the original position of his "I," and then to begin the process all over again *ad nauseum*. This role-switching, in turn, forces us to reexamine the static I-centric understanding of the literary object itself. Through this process, it becomes possible to turn you and I as that other you and that oher I. Using parenthetical asides in the stream of the narration Yi adopts various opposing views, both making comments and commenting on the nature of com-menting itself: in the case of "here(there)," he observes this here from a distance in order to prevent assimilation into his own "here," while saying, "imagining you (imagining the me that is imagining you)," problematizes the very premise of the "I" as the subject considering the object. All of this, in turn, reveals the ways in which literary truth can defy conclusion itself.

Jeong Hye-gyeong

어올리기도 꼬집기도 하면서 넋을 송두리째 흔들고 빼어놓을 필요가 있었다. 독자를 주눅 들게 하고, 묵사발을 만듦으로써 소설 쓰기의 자유랄까, 또 말해 불발의 성스러움을 얻어내고자 하는 전략이 깔려 있었다고나 할까.

김윤식

"What is writing fiction, and what is its significance, and what must be done to make it possible?" For author Yi In-seong, the first and foremost question has always been the analysis of the "literary reader." This is a project that requires him to be both threatening and comforting, to raise up but also to pinch the reader, to shake the spirit whole and to wrench it out of itself. To intimidate the reader; to crush story into pulp for the freedom of writing itself. To extract the sacred from the undetonated explosive. We could say that these are the underlying strategies here.

Kim Yun-sik

이인성

이인성은 1953년 12월 9일 서울에서 태어나 줄곧 서울에서 살아왔다. 대학에서는 프랑스 연극을 전공하고 그 연구자로서의 길을 병행해 걸어온 그는 1983~1988년에 한국외국어대학 불어과와 1989~2006년에 서울대학교 불문과 교수로 재직한 바 있다.

어린 시절부터 학자 가문의 계몽주의적 분위기에 영향을 받으며 성장한 그는, 그러나 청소년기를 거치며 탐미적 문학과 예술에 빠져들어 글쓰기에 몰두하기 시작했다. 1973년 서울대학교 불문학과에 입학한 뒤, 그는 기성 문단의 폐쇄성과 관습에서 벗어나 자유로운 글쓰기를 지향하는 문우들과《언어 탐구》라는 동인지를 간행하면서 실험적인 희곡·소설들을 발표하기도 했는데, 이는 그가 미래의 작가 활동을 본격화시키는 계기가 되었다.

문학적 자유를 추구하는 그의 일관된 태도는, 1980년 계간《문학과지성》을 통해 공식적으로 문단에 발을 디딘 이후에도, 문학 그 자체로 억압적 시대에 응전하

Yi In-seong

Born in the city on December 9th, 1953, Yi In-seong lives in Seoul to this day. After studying French Drama in university, Yi went on to hold professorships in the French Department at Hanguk University of Foreign Studies (1983-1988) and the French Literature Department at Seoul National University (1989-2006).

Having grown up under the influence of a family of academic intellectuals, the adolescent Yi nevertheless came to embrace aestheticism in art and literature and began to concentrate on his own writing. After enrolling in the French Literature department at Seoul National University in 1973, Yi came together with like-minded friends who shared his vision of a freer kind of writing, something beyond the customs and conventions of the restrictive literary establishment, and established the literary magazine *Linguistic Explorations*. It was during this period, between founding this journal and printing several of his own experimental plays and stories in it, that Yi's future as an author began to take shape.

자는 기치를 내걸고 시인 이성복, 평론가 정과리와 함께 부정기 문학지(무크지)《우리 세대의 문학》을 발간하는 '소집단 문학 운동'으로 발전하였다. 2001년에 문화적 상업주의의 범람에 맞서 문학의 자율적 위치를 확립하기 위해 계간《문학·판》을 창간했던 것도 같은 맥락에서 이해될 수 있다.

과작의 작가인 그는 1983년에 첫 연작 장편 『낯선 시간 속으로』를 출간하였다. 그가 만들어낸 독창적 문학 세계의 원형으로 간주되는 이 작품에서 엿보여진, 의식의 심연을 탐험하는 실험적 글쓰기와 구성 방식은 이후의 작품들에서 지속적으로 심화되었다. 예를 들어 두 번째 연작 장편 『한없이 낮은 숨결』(1987)은, 각 부분이 독립적으로 분절되어 있으면서도 동시에 하나의 전체로 얽히는 구성 방식을 다성적 목소리를 통해 더욱 정교하게 구축하고 있으며, 장편 『미쳐버리고 싶은, 미쳐지지 않는』(1995)은 인칭과 시제의 분할에 대응하는 네 개의 문체를 구사하는 글쓰기 방식으로 나아갔다. 자신의 창작 방법론에 대한 그의 숙고는 그의 문학 에세이 집 『식물성의 저항』(2000)에 표명되어 있으며, 그러한 문학적 탐구는 그가 『강어귀에 섬 하나』(1999) 이후 오

Even after making his official literary debut in 1980 via publication of his fiction in the quarterly *Literature and Intelligence* from Moonji Publishing, Yi did not stray from this vision of literary freedom; in 1982, Yi joined forces with poet Lee Seong-bok and critic Jeong Gwa-li and, united by their belief in the power of literature to challenge the realities of an oppressive age, put out *The Literature of Our Generation*, a one-off publication that became the first act of their 'Small-Group Literary Activism.' Indeed, even Yi's founding of *Munhak Pan* (Literary Scene) in 2001 can be understood as a continuation of this original vision, as the journal is meant to serve as a platform where literature can stand autonomous, a bulwark against the current deluge of commercialism in contemporary literature.

More tortoise than hare when it comes to publishing, Yi made his literary debut with his first serialied novel, *Into Unfamiliar Time*, in 1983. Widely considered to be archetypal of the inventive and original literary landscapes Yi creates, this work also provides a glimpse of the author's experimental use of language and structure as tools to explore the abyss of human consciousness—an ongoing and overarching project that has carried

랜만에 다시 펴내는 새로운 연작 장편『악몽 소설』(2013년 근간, 이 작품의 주요 부분을 구성할 네 개의 이야기는 그 사이에 이미 문학잡지에 발표되었다)에서도 변함없이 계속되고 있다. 그의 작품들은 한국적 전위 문학의 대표적인 예로 간주되어, 프랑스어, 스페인어, 독일어, 중국어 등 여러 언어로 활발하게 번역되고 있다.

through his subsequent works, only deepening in scope and scale with time. For example, Yi's second serialized novel, *The Shallowest Breath* (1987), boasts an intricately constructed scaffolding of multiple voices that illuminate an internal structure of free-standing sections that also come together into a tangled whole; meanwhile, Yi's next novel, *Insanity Desired; Insanity Denied* (1995) is written in four distinct prose styles as a direct response to the generally accepted division between verb tense agreement and point of view. Yi's reflections on his own creative process can be found in *The Vegetative Resistance* (2000), his collection of essays, and with his newest serialized novel *Nightmare Fiction* (2013), his first publication since 1999's *An Island At The River's Mouth*, his ongoing literary explorations continue unabated.

Because his works are considered to be representative of avant-garde Korean literature writ large, Yi In-seong's stories and novels have been and continue to be actively translated into numerous different languages, including French, Spanish, German, and Chinese.

번역 **마야 웨스트** Translated by Maya West

리드 대학교를 졸업했고 2003년 한국 문학 번역원 신인상을 탔다. 현재 서울에 거주하며 프리랜서 작가, 번역가로 활동하고 있다.

Maya West, graduate of Reed College and recipient of the 2003 Korean Literature Translation Institute's Grand Prize for New Translators, currently lives and works in Seoul as a freelance writer and translator.

감수 **전승희, 데이비드 윌리엄 홍**
Edited by Jeon Seung-hee and David William Hong

전승희는 서울대학교와 하버드대학교에서 영문학과 비교문학으로 박사 학위를 받았으며, 현재 하버드대학교 한국학 연구소의 연구원으로 재직하며 아시아 문예 계간지 《ASIA》 편집위원으로 활동 중이다. 현대 한국문학 및 세계문학을 다룬 논문을 다수 발표했으며, 바흐친의 『장편소설과 민중언어』, 제인 오스틴의 『오만과 편견』 등을 공역했다. 1988년 한국여성연구소의 창립과 《여성과 사회》의 창간에 참여했고, 2002년부터 보스턴 지역 피학대 여성을 위한 단체인 '트랜지션하우스' 운영에 참여해 왔다. 2006년 하버드대학교 한국학 연구소에서 '한국 현대사와 기억'을 주제로 한 워크숍을 주관했다.

Jeon Seung-hee is a member of the Editorial Board of ASIA, is a Fellow at the Korea Institute, Harvard University. She received a Ph.D. in English Literature from Seoul National University and a Ph.D. in Comparative Literature from Harvard University. She has presented and published numerous papers on modern Korean and world literature. She is also a co-translator of Mikhail Bakhtin's *Novel and the People's Culture* and Jane Austen's *Pride and Prejudice*. She is a founding member of the Korean Women's Studies Institute and of the biannual Women's Studies' journal *Women and Society* (1988), and she has been working at 'Transition House,' the first and oldest shelter for battered women in New England. She organized a workshop entitled "The Politics of Memory in Modern Korea" at the Korea Institute, Harvard University, in 2006. She also served as an advising committee member for the Asia-Africa Literature Festival in 2007 and for the POSCO Asian Literature Forum in 2008.

데이비드 윌리엄 홍은 미국 일리노이주 시카고에서 태어났다. 일리노이대학교에서 영문학을, 뉴욕대학교에서 영어교육을 공부했다. 지난 2년간 서울에 거주하면서 처음으로 한국인과 아시아계 미국인 문학에 깊이 몰두할 기회를 가졌다. 현재 뉴욕에서 거주하며 강의와 저술 활동을 한다.

David William Hong was born in 1986 in Chicago, Illinois. He studied English Literature at the University of Illinois and English Education at New York University. For the past two years, he lived in Seoul, South Korea, where he was able to immerse himself in Korean and Asian-American literature for the first time. Currently, he lives in New York City, teaching and writing.

바이링궐 에디션 한국 대표 소설 043
당신에 대해서

2013년 10월 18일 초판 1쇄 인쇄 | 2013년 10월 25일 초판 1쇄 발행

지은이 이인성 | 옮긴이 마야 웨스트 | 펴낸이 방재석
감수 전승희, 데이비드 윌리엄 홍 | 기획 정은경, 전성태, 이경재
편집 정수인, 이은혜 | 관리 박신영 | 디자인 이춘희
펴낸곳 아시아 | 출판등록 2006년 1월 31일 제319-2006-4호
주소 서울특별시 동작구 흑석동 100-16
전화 02.821.5055 | 팩스 02.821.5057 | 홈페이지 www.bookasia.org
ISBN 978-89-94006-94-9 (set) | 978-89-94006-06-2 (04810)
값은 뒤표지에 있습니다.

Bi-lingual Edition Modern Korean Literature 043
On You

Written by Yi In-seong | Translated by Maya West
Published by Asia Publishers | 100-16 Heukseok-dong, Dongjak-gu, Seoul, Korea
Homepage Address www.bookasia.org | Tel. (822).821.5055 | Fax. (822).821.5057
First published in Korea by Asia Publishers 2013
ISBN 978-89-94006-94-9 (set) | 978-89-94006-06-2 (04810)